The Ultimate
BQC
Book of Knowledge

Derek O'Brien was born in Kolkata. He began his professional career as a journalist for *Sportsworld* magazine but soon shifted to advertising. After working for a number of very successful years as Creative Head of Ogilvy, Derek decided to focus all his energy and talent in his passion—quizzing.

Today, Derek O'Brien is Asia's best-known quizmaster and the CEO of Derek O'Brien & Associates. He is the host of the longest-running game show on Indian television, the Bournvita Quiz Contest, for which he was voted the Best Anchor of a Game Show at the Indian Television Academy Awards for three years in a row. He also hosts the longest-running corporate quiz show, the Economic Times Brand Equity Quiz. Always innovating and keeping abreast with the times, Derek is also credited with having conducted the first quiz on Twitter in 2010.

Derek O'Brien has written several best-selling reference and quiz books. He is also the author of two extremely successful school textbook series, *Know and Grow with Derek* and *Be a GK Champ*.

In 2011, Derek O'Brien was voted to the Rajya Sabha as a Member of Parliament (MP).

THE ULTIMATE

BOOK OF KNOWLEDGE

VOLUME 1

DEREK O'BRIEN

RUPA

Published by
Rupa Publications India Pvt. Ltd 2012
7/16, Ansari Road, Daryaganj
New Delhi 110002

Sales Centres:

Allahabad Bengaluru Chennai
Hyderabad Jaipur Kathmandu
Kolkata Mumbai

ISBN 978-81-291-2038-0

Fifth impression 2015

10 9 8 7 6 5

CONTENTS

FOREWORD

As we celebrate forty incredible years of the Bournvita Quiz Contest this year, it gives me immense pleasure in introducing to you *The Ultimate Bournvita Quiz Contest Book of Knowledge*.

Since its launch in 1948, Cadbury Bournvita has been one of India's most loved and trusted brands. For over six decades, the brand has been an enduring symbol of mental and physical health and all-round development. In 1972, Cadbury India introduced the Bournvita Quiz Contest (BQC) as a radio programme. Following its tremendous success on radio, the programme found a new avatar on television in 1994. After a hiatus of a few years and following the compelling public movement to 'Bring back BQC', 2011 saw the return of India's favourite quiz contest to national television.

During the last forty years, this show has touched the lives of over 12 lakh children and millions of loyal viewers through its 600+ television episodes. A number of reputed personalities and celebrities from the fields of cinema, music, sports and politics have also made special appearances on the show.

The Ultimate Bournvita Quiz Contest Book of

Knowledge comes to you in two volumes, with a compilation of questions asked on BQC from 1994 to 2010. So if you think you have an unquenchable thirst for knowledge, an openness to learn anything new and a knack for facts, I am sure you will enjoy this book!

I would like to take this opportunity to thank the team from Derek O'Brien & Associates for producing this book. I would also like to thank the millions of viewers, students, principals and teachers for their love and support, which in turn has made the Bournvita Quiz Contest a household name!

Happy quizzing!

Anand Kripalu
President, India & South East Asia
Cadbury India Limited

INTRODUCTION

The Bournvita Quiz Contest (BQC) made its debut as a radio programme in 1972. From radio it moved to television in 1994, and has been a part of our lives for nearly forty years now. Over the years, as the show won multiple awards for Best Children's programme and Best Host, my team and I have lived and grown with it. To celebrate these decades of making knowledge fun, we bring you an exhaustive compilation of questions in two volumes. In *The Ultimate Bournvita Quiz Contest Book of Knowledge* Volumes 1 and 2, we have brought together over 3,000 questions asked on television, from the very first show in 1994 right until 2010.

It has been great fun, yet hard work, putting together these two volumes. My colleagues and I have burnt the proverbial midnight oil, while enjoying the nostalgia of sifting through stacks of old questions and looking through hours of tapes. So much has changed over the years, since 1994: the participants, the sets, the format, even the way I look...I have the very able and stunning Saumya Tandon as co-quizmaster now, and we have gone bilingual. But the very core of the Bournvita Quiz Contest, which is a quiz with a simple, uncomplicated and classic format, has remained untouched. And that is what makes BQC special!

The questions included in these two volumes are ones we felt would always entertain and educate students and quiz lovers. I have loved asking each one of these questions, and hope you will enjoy reading them too.

Thank you!

With every good wish,

Derek O'Brien

P.S. Stay in touch with me through www.twitter.com, my handle is @quizderek.

HALL OF FAME

PAST WINNERS OF THE BOURNVITA
QUIZ CONTEST

1994–1995, Mumbai
Campion High School, Mumbai
Balakrishnan Sivaraman, Sudhanshu Bhuwalka

1995–1996, Mumbai
Kendriya Vidyalaya, Powai, Mumbai
Eipy Koshy, Gourav Shah

1996–1997, Mumbai
Bombay International High School, Mumbai
Nirica Borges, Advait Behara

1997, Mumbai
Mount Saint Mary's School, New Delhi
Joe Christy, Maninder Singh Jessel

1997–1998, Mumbai
Bombay Scottish High School, Mumbai
Shaambhavi Pandyaa, Rahul Lalmalani

1998, Mumbai
Sacred Heart Convent School, Jamshedpur
Ela Verma, Lavanya Raghavan

1998–1999, Mumbai
Indian School Al Ghubra, Muscat
Anand Raghavan, Hitesh Kanvatirtha

1999, Mumbai
Maneckji Cooper High School, Mumbai
Ipsita Bandopadhyay, Gourav Bhattacharya

1999–2000, Mumbai
Chettinad Vidyashram, Chennai
Siddharth, Karthik Das

2000–2001, Mumbai
Bharatiya Vidya Bhavan, Hyderabad
Ananya Bhaskar, Aksha Anand

2001 September, Mumbai
Brightlands, Dehradun
Ankur Bharadwaj, Shray Sharma

2001 December, Mumbai
Little Flower High School, Hyderabad
G. Mithilesh, K. Siddharth Reddy

2002 February, Bentota, Sri Lanka
G.D. Birla Centre For Education, Kolkata
Namrata Basu, Rituparna Dey

2002 June, Mumbai
Kerala Samajam Public School, Jamshedpur
Saurav Biswas, Kunal Mohan

2002 September, Mumbai
Jamnabai Narsee School, Mumbai
Sharan Narayanan, Vishnu Shrest

2003 January, Kerala
Naval Public High School, Mumbai
Apoorva Sharma, Abhishek Pandit

2003 May, Kolkata
St Patrick's Higher Secondary School, Asansol
Pushpen Dasgupta, Shamik Ray

2003 October, Sangla
St Agnes Loreto Day School, Lucknow
Aastha Srivastava, Illa Gupta

2004 February, Swabhumi, Kolkata
Apeejay School, Jalandhar
Mohit Thukral, Sahil Sareen

2004 May, Goa
Springdales School, Delhi
Anirudh Sridhar, B. Anuraag

2004 July, Indian Military Academy, Dehradun
The Mother's International School, Delhi
Krittika Adhikary, Milind Ganjoo

2004 November, Kolkata
Amity International School, New Delhi
Aishwarya Singhal, Adarsh Modi

2005 February, Kolkata
St Kabir, Ahmedabad
Yogarshi Vyas, Helish Sharma

2005 May, Kolkata
Brightlands, Dehradun
Akshay Sharma, Avantika Singh

2005 August, Kolkata
Amity International, New Delhi
Utkarsh Johari, Aishwarya Singhal

2006 July, Kolkata
Riverdale High School, Dehradun
Kartikeya Panwar, Sumit Nair

2006 November, Kolkata
Seth Jaipuria School, Lucknow
Ratnaksha Lele, Ananya Kumar Singh

2011 August, Kolkata
Amity International School, Noida
Kripi Badonia, Shinjini Biswas

2012 January, Kolkata
Birla Vidya Niketan, New Delhi
Anusha Malhotra, Nitya Bansal

CREDITS

DIRECTOR	Derek O'Brien
CO-QUIZMASTER	Saumya Tandon
CREATIVE DIRECTOR	Shrradha Kulkarni
EXECUTIVE PRODUCERS	Andrew Scolt
	Nayan Chaudhury
	Sunil Shah
PRODUCER	Prabuddha Chatterjee (Gulu)
ONLINE DIRECTOR	Dongrej Gor
DOP	R. Diwakaran
SOUND	Ashwyn Balsaver
	Seby Fernandes
SENIOR ASSOCIATES, RESEARCH	Amit Ghosh
	Shalini Chaudhury
ASSOCIATES, RESEARCH	Anik Ghosal
	Srirupa Roy
	Ayashman Dey
	Nilanjana Basu
	Ammar Hamid
	Natasha Gasper
SENIOR RELATIONSHIP ASSOCIATES	Shane Alliew
	Heena Ade (Israni)

RELATIONSHIP ASSOCIATES	Fatema Marfatia
	Calvin Tully
	Laressa Gomez
	Sean Augustine
	Durjoy Guha
	Dipankar Rao
	Conrad Pote
	Sheldon Alliew
	Ishita Bose Chakraborty
	Aubrey Whyte
	Daniel Johns
	Fionna Sayers
	Michael Blacquiere
	Tapan Roy
SENIOR ASSOCIATE, FINANCE	Kalyanmoy Hazra
PRODUCTION ASSOCIATES	Sreevalsa Menon
	Shane Baptiste
	Vinu Joseph
	Supriyo Nandi
	Victor Bhat
SENIOR ASSOCIATE, DESIGN	Mahua Basu
SAUMYA'S HAIR & MAKE-UP ARTIST	Elton Fernandez
SAUMYA'S WARDROBE	Kiran Uttam Ghosh
OPERATIVE	B. Lokabiraman
CAMERAMEN	Bhagyawan
	Anandan
	D. Nandakumar
	Debabrata Paul
	Sridhar

HINDI SCRIPT	Rajneesh Kaushal
OFFLINE EDITORS	Vivek Iyer
	Bhavin Patel
JIMMY JIB	Arshad Shaikh
	Saleem Syed
MUSIC	Shankar, Ehsaan, Loy
ASST TO DOP	Selvaraj Xavier
	J. Selvam
SET DESIGN & FABRICATION	Kosmos India
IID EQUIPMENT	Kaliedoxcope
SOUND, LIGHTS & AV	Friends Of Shiva
SHOT AT	Aurora Studio
PRODUCTION ASSISTANTS	Pabitra
	Mrinal
	Saha
	Jha
	Sudip
MAKE-UP	Babu

INDIA

1. Which Indian state was called North-East Frontier Agency till 1972?
2. Which observatory did Sawai Jai Singh build at Delhi, Jaipur, Varanasi, Mathura and Ujjain?
3. Who was the first Indian to receive both the Nobel Prize and the Bharat Ratna?
4. Which musical instrument is also known as venu, vamsi, murali, pillankarovi and kolalu?
5. Which Hindu statesman, also known as Vishnugupta, was Chandragupta Maurya's main counsellor and advisor?
6. What was carried in a third class train compartment numbered 2949 on 12 February 1948 to the Triveni, Allahabad?
7. Who was the first Indian to win the Miss Universe title?
8. Who built the famous Buland Darwaza to commemorate his victory in Gujarat?
9. In India, which Mumbai-born politician's birth anniversary is celebrated as Sadbhavna Diwas and death anniversary as Anti-Terrorism Day?
10. The capital of which Indian state is named after

Ananthan, the cosmic serpent with a thousand heads?

11. Upon completion in 1931, it was called the All India War Memorial. How do we know it today?

12. Which famous landmark was built in the thirteenth century by King Narasimhadeva in the shape of a chariot with twenty-four wheels, drawn by seven horses?

13. Which two words are inscribed below the abacus on the Emblem of India?

14. Which famous song, composed by Muhammad Iqbal, is also known as 'Tarana-e-Hindi'?

15. Which festival connects Bohag or Rongali, Kati or Kangali, and Magh or Bhogali?

16. In which state is the Keoladeo National Park located?

17. In 1661, which Indian city was given to Great Britain by Portugal as part of the dowry at the marriage of Catherine of Braganza to Charles II?

18. After which famous historical leader is the capital of Gujarat named?

19. In 1984, Rakesh Sharma went into space and Bachendri Pal became the first Indian woman to climb Mount Everest. What started for the first time in Kolkata, and indeed in India, on 24 October 1984?

20. Akoori is a traditional dish of which community?

21. With which classical dance form would you associate the name of Birju Maharaj?

22. *The Story of My Life* is the autobiography of the first non-Congress prime minister of independent India. Name him.

23. Which city derives its name from Amrit Sarovar, the holy tank that surrounds Sri Harmandir Sahib?

24. 'Yakshagana' is a traditional theatre form of which Indian state?
25. Which is the senior-most regiment in the Indian Army?
26. Who was issued India's first pilot's licence in 1929?
27. If Shah Jahan built the Taj Mahal, who built the Jama Masjid in Delhi?
28. In 1974, who became the first Indian woman singer to receive the Ramon Magsaysay award?
29. Which Indian state was previously called the United Provinces?
30. *Ficus religiosa* is the scientific name of which tree?
31. Which state in India has the largest number of seats in the Lok Sabha?
32. Which Nobel Prize winner was a teacher at St Mary's High School, Kolkata, from 1931 to 1948?
33. Who launched the 'Bharat Jodo' or 'Knit India' movement from Kashmir to Kanyakumari in 1985?
34. What is the state tree of Kerala?
35. Indira Gandhi was the first woman prime minister of India. Who was the first woman to sit on the throne of Delhi?
36. In 1448, who built the tower known as Vijaya Stambha at Chittorgarh Fort?
37. In India, how many digits comprise the PNR number on a railway ticket?
38. *Raga Mala* is the autobiography of which famous Indian musician?
39. It is called turmeric in English. What is it called in Hindi?
40. If Vishakhapatnam is in Andhra Pradesh, in which state is Vijayawada?

41. What came into being on 7 July 1948 as the first multipurpose river valley project of independent India?
42. Who was the famous Indian occupant of Soyuz T-11?
43. With which cartoonist would you associate the 'You Said It' series?
44. Which mode of transport was discontinued in Chennai on 11 April 1953?
45. In which Indian state is the famous Bolgatty Palace located?
46. According to S. Radhakrishnan, which colour on the National Flag of India denotes our relation to soil and plant life?
47. Kurukshetra and Panipat are districts of which state of India?
48. Bahadur Shah II was the last ruler of which dynasty?
49. According to Lokmanya Tilak's famous slogan, what was his birthright?
50. In which state is the famous Pushkar fair held?

Answers on pages 125–126

GEOGRAPHY

1. Which Indian city was formerly called Pataligram, Kusumpur and Azeemabad?
2. K2 or Godwin Austen is the world's second highest peak. To which range of mountains does it belong?
3. The name of which country, situated in both Europe and Asia, is also the name of a bird?
4. In 1590, the Portuguese first sighted the island of Taiwan. What did they name it?
5. Till 1961, by what name was the city of Volgograd known?
6. In which capital city would you find the famous Temple of the Emerald Buddha?
7. Which Asian country in the Pacific Ocean is made up of 7,107 islands, the largest of them being Luzon?
8. The flag of which country depicts a crossed rifle and hoe in black superimposed on an open white book?
9. In which continent is the Sahara desert?
10. 'Checkpoint Charlie' was a checkpoint on the border of which two European cities? (Hint: The checkpoint no longer exists.)
11. The Bronx, Brooklyn, Queens, Staten Island and Manhattan together form which city?

12. In which country would you drive down an autobahn?

13. The Malvinas Islands was the centre of a war against Great Britain in the early eighties. How do we know them better?

14. Which capital city was known to the Romans as Lutetia? (Hint: Think Asterix!)

15. Sometimes described as a white snake, which glacier is often regarded as the world's highest battleground?

16. Which is the longest of the five tributaries of the Indus river?

17. The word 'Helvetia' appears on the stamps of which country?

18. Which country's population consists mostly of Flemings and Walloons?

19. What is common to the following: Anjuna, Baga, Calangute and Vagator?

20. The capital of which African country is named after the US president James Monroe?

21. What name did Erik the Red give to a large island with fertile green valleys he had discovered in 982 CE?

22. Which desert covers almost all of Botswana?

23. Which river, called Nahr Al-Urdun in Arabic, shares its name with an Arab country of southwest Asia?

24. Which is the largest country in the world in terms of area?

25. How many colours does the South African flag display?

26. Which cartographer introduced the term 'atlas' for a collection of maps?

27. Which geographical feature shares its name with the fourth letter of the Greek alphabet?

28. What island did Peter Minuit acquire for sixty guilders from the Native Americans?
29. Which mountain is often referred to as the backbone of South America?
30. Beside which river does the city of Baghdad lie?
31. Cirrus, cirrocumulus, stratus and nimbostratus are types of what?
32. The capital of which Scandinavian country is located primarily on the island of Zealand?
33. The name of which country was coined by Choudhry Rahmat Ali and is said to be an acronym formed from Punjab, Afghania, Kashmir, Sind and Baluchistan?
34. What did Gutzon Borglum and his son Lincoln leave behind in the Black Hills of South Dakota, USA?
35. Tanzania was formed by the merger of which two sovereign states?
36. The Russians know this as Kaspiyskoye More. How is it known to us?
37. The Great Sphinx at Giza in Egypt has a human head and the body of which animal?
38. On which African river is the Victoria Falls located?
39. If you were visiting the archaeological areas of Pompeii, Herculaneum and Torre Annunziata, which country would you be in?
40. The name of the main airport of which city was changed from Idlewild to John F. Kennedy?
41. The Dead Sea lies between Israel and which other country?
42. In which country is Bastille Day a national holiday?
43. Which city would you be in if you passed under the famous Bridge of Sighs?

44. What is the colour of the Golden Gate Bridge in San Francisco?
45. Which is the southernmost capital city in the world?
46. In which continent are the Prince Charles Mountains located?
47. King Khalid International Airport serves which city?
48. This city was known as Saigon until 1976. What is it called today?
49. The Suez Canal is an artificial waterway connecting the Red Sea with which sea?
50. Which river is the largest drainage system in the world in terms of the volume of its flow and the area of its basin?

Answers on pages 127–128

ENTERTAINMENT

1. I was popularly known as M.S. I was born in Madurai. I received the Bharat Ratna in 1998. Who am I?
2. Which actress won her first National Award for Best Actress for the 1974 film *Ankur*?
3. Which Navratna in Akbar's court is said to have created the ragas 'Miyan Malhar' and 'Miyan ki Todi'?
4. Which crime fighter's parents were killed by Joe 'Chill' Chilton?
5. Who has published a scrapbook of poems and prose about dancing, the universe, dolphins, his mother and God, titled *Dancing the Dream*?
6. Name the music composer for the following films: *Pather Panchali, Aparajito* and *Apur Sansar.*
7. Who played the role of Itzhak Stern in the 1993 film *Schindler's List*?
8. Name the American president and his wife who acted in the 1957 film *Hellcats of the Navy.*
9. In fiction, what was the name of the park that John Hammond built on Isla Nublar, off the Costa Rican coast?
10. What is a rockumentary?

11. Who played the role of Wajid Ali Shah in the 1977 film *Shatranj Ke Khiladi*?

12. Who was the first recipient of the Dadasaheb Phalke Award?

13. What was the name of Hema Malini's horse in the 1975 film *Sholay*?

14. Name the Hollywood actor who shares his surname with a car manufacturing company, and is famous for his role as an archaeologist named Dr Jones.

15. Which film by Satyajit Ray was completed when Dr B.C. Roy, former chief minister of West Bengal, provided funds from the Public Works Department, on the grounds that path (road) was a matter within the PWD's jurisdiction?

16. In the film *The Lion King*, Simba was a lion. What kind of a creature was Timon?

17. Which famous director wrote the story of the 1958 film *Madhumati*?

18. In *Asterix and the Magic Carpet*, what was the name of the fakir on whose carpet Asterix and Obelix travelled to India?

19. Which cartoon character has nephews named Huey, Dewey and Louie?

20. In Tintin comics, Snowy is afraid of only one creature. What is it?

21. My father won a Padma Bhushan in 1976, my wife won a Padma Shri in 1992 and I have received a Padma Shri and a Padma Bhushan. Who am I?

22. If a killer whale was the titular character in the film *Free Willy*, then what was the titular animal in the film *Flipper*?

23. In 1962, which actor was born as Thomas Mapother IV?

24. Which cricketer played the role of a villain with a bald pate in the film *Kabhi Ajnabi The*?

25. In cartoons, who are Brain, Choo Choo, Spook, Fancy Fancy and Benny the Ball?

26. Which character did actor Leonard Nimoy portray in *Star Trek V: The Final Frontier*?

27. Who played the role of Kevin McCallister in the 1990 film *Home Alone*?

28. Which Hollywood 1956 classic has the line, 'So let it be written, so it shall be done'?

29. We were born as Arthur Stanley Jefferson and Oliver Norvell Hardy. We are a famous comedy pair. How are we better known?

30. Which actor won the National Award for Best Actor twice, for *Dastak* in 1971 and *Koshish* in 1973?

31. Who became the youngest percussionist to be awarded the Padma Shri in 1988, and the Padma Bhushan in 2002?

32. Who composed the music for the 1969 film *Goopy Gyne Bagha Byne*?

33. The famous singer Lucky Ali's father was an actor. Name him.

34. The English title of the dubbed version of which 1989 film was *When Love Calls*?

35. What is the term used to describe an entertainer who makes a wooden dummy appear to speak?

36. Which 1992 animated film had the tagline 'Imagine if you had three wishes, three hopes, three dreams and they all could come true'?

37. In cartoons, what tattoo does Popeye have on his forearm?
38. Which fictional character has a boss named M, whose secretary is called Miss Moneypenny?
39. Which musician played the role of Inder Lal in the 1983 film *Heat and Dust*?
40. In which film would you meet these seven children: Liesl, Louisa, Friedrich, Kurt, Brigitta, Marta and Gretl?
41. Which actor made his debut in a lead role opposite Mamata Shankar in Mrinal Sen's *Mrigaya*?
42. Amitabh Bachchan plays the role of the father in the film *Mahaan*. Who plays the role of his twin sons?
43. Who was the first actor to appear on the cover of *Time* magazine?
44. Which famous actress played the role of Irene in the 1975 film *Julie*?
45. Kedarnath Bhattacharya is a popular singer. By what name do we know him better?
46. According to the 2005 *Guinness Book of World Records*, which film, made in 1982, had the most extras?
47. Who played the title role in the 1959 film *Ben-Hur*?
48. Which Indian film director was awarded the 1967 Ramon Magsaysay Award for Journalism, Literature and Creative Communication Arts?
49. What is Mr Plod's profession in the Noddy books?
50. I played a blind school principal in the 1980 film *Sparsh* and a professor in the 1993 film *Sir*. Who am I?

Answers on pages 128–130

1. She lives in St Mary Mead.
2. Kleptomaniac
3. Datum
4. Albumen
5. Ranko the gorilla appeared in this Tintin adventure.
6. It is called a drey.
7. Isohyet
8. Silk Route
9. The Heartbreak Kid
10. Epitaph
11. He is assisted by a group of fellow outlaws known as the 'Merry Men'.
12. Workers, drones and queens
13. Dadamoni
14. Anemometer
15. The first Swede male tennis player to become world number one in the Open era.
16. It is an arrangement of straps placed over an animal's snout.
17. It is a curved piece of wood that can be thrown so that it will return to the thrower, traditionally used by Australian Aborigines as a hunting weapon.

18. It was built by Gustave Eiffel for the Universal Exposition of 1889 celebrating the centenary of the French Revolution.
19. Boxing Day
20. Jellystone National Park
21. It is a piece of paper which indicates that you have paid for something.
22. Hypotenuse
23. A.S. Dileep Kumar (Hint: Music)
24. In the Ramayana, she was Lakshmana and Shatrughna's mother.
25. Aqua regia
26. Duodenum, jejunum and ileum
27. This husk, used to aid digestion, is commercially produced from *P. ovata* and *P. psyllium* in Pakistan and India.
28. This device is a blend of a modulator and a demodulator.
29. Talons
30. This tool is called a jack.
31. In *Winnie the Pooh*, she is Roo's mother.
32. He made his directorial debut with *Kuch Kuch Hota Hai.*
33. Harmattan
34. Varicella
35. The author of *A House for Mr Biswas*
36. In Western astrology, it is the second sign of the zodiac.
37. Mezzanine
38. Howard Carter
39. This country was once known as South West Africa.

40. Hydrophobia is its other name.
41. This is where leather is produced from animal skins.
42. It was the last capital of the kingdom of Vijayanagar.
43. Collage
44. In a 1982 film he came to Earth and wanted to call home.
45. The SI unit of energy or work is named after this scientist.
46. Anastasia and Drizella (Hint: Children's literature)
47. This J-shaped elastic sac is the widest part of the digestive system.
48. In comics, Lothar is his best friend and crime-fighting companion.
49. Hellas
50. Chandigarh was planned by this French architect.

Answers on pages 130–132

FUN FACTS 1

1. The Peregrine falcon is the fastest bird in the sky. It can dive towards the Earth at more than 200 miles per hour.
2. Harold Sakata, who played the role of 'Oddjob' in the James Bond film *Goldfinger*, won a silver medal in weightlifting at the 1948 Summer Olympics.
3. The last private resident of No. 10 Downing Street was called Mr Chicken.
4. Barren Island, situated 135 km from Port Blair, is the only active volcano in India.
5. The Rowlatt Bill denied civil liberties to Indians. It was this bill that drew Mahatma Gandhi into active Indian politics.
6. Kedgeree, a dish that originated among the British colonials in India, was derived from the Indian dish khichdi, made from rice, lentils, onions and spices.
7. A year on Venus lasts for 335 Earth days, a month shorter than Earth's, as it is closer to the sun than we are.
8. *Shatranj Ke Khiladi* was Satyajit Ray's first Hindi film. Set in Lucknow, just before the Indian Mutiny, it depicts the downfall of the ruler Wajid Ali Shah.

9. Leonardo da Vinci had painted several portraits during his stay at Florence, but the only one that survives is the famous 'Mona Lisa'.
10. The peafowl is considered sacred in Indian mythology as Kartikeya, son of Shiva and Parvati, rides on its back.
11. Old Birla House on 5, Tees January Marg, New Delhi, was where Mahatma Gandhi spent the last 144 days of his life, and is now a museum.
12. African elephants use two finger-like features at the end of their trunks to grab small items. Asian elephants have one of these.

MIXED BAG 1

1. According to the most prevalent story, what mode of transport did Jonathan Scobie, an American missionary, invent in 1869?
2. On which famous street is the New York Stock Exchange located?
3. Which prime minister of India wrote the book *The Insider*?
4. Which mountain was previously referred to as Peak XV by surveyors?
5. A hinny is a hybrid offspring of which two animals?
6. Which Mughal emperor planted 1,00,000 mango trees in Darbhanga, Bihar at a place now known as Lakhi Bagh?
7. The name of the film *Do Bigha Zamin*, directed by Bimal Roy, was actually a poem written by whom?
8. Crisscross words is an earlier version of which board game?
9. What nickname is common to Venkatapathy Raju, tennis player Ken Rosewall and actor Jean-Claude Van Damme?
10. The story of which novel revolves around the fortunes of four families: the Mehras, the Kapoors, the Khans and the Chatterjis?

11. What does OMOV mean in terms of voting in many democratic countries?

12. Tussar, Muga and Endi are varieties of what?

13. What profession connects Roland Garros, Rajiv Gandhi and Vijaypat Singhania?

14. What part of a car engine is called a muffler in the US?

15. In 1995, Christopher Pile or the Black Baron, was convicted of what?

16. Why were copper rivets put on denim jeans?

17. On which part of the body is a mitten worn?

18. Which six-letter word meaning a large bowl-shaped cavity in the ground or on the surface of a planet comes from a Greek word meaning 'mixing bowl'?

19. Who is common to Dasher, Dancer, Prancer, Vixen, Comet, Cupid, Donner/Donder, Blitzen and Rudolph?

20. The Swiss Guards are responsible for the safety of which religious head?

21. What kind of vehicle was sometimes referred to as 'Black Maria'?

22. What was the code name of the secret project to develop atomic bombs during World War II in the US?

23. Which famous dancer founded Kalakshetra at Adyar in Chennai?

24. What is the first month of the Gregorian calendar?

25. What kind of a creature is Jerry in the cartoon series Tom and Jerry?

26. On which part of your body would you wear a kippah?

27. The sound of an elephant can be associated with which musical instrument?

28. The famous Sun Temple of Modhera is located in which state?

29. What do the number of dots on all six faces of a dice add up to?

30. The word 'hygiene' is named after the Greek goddess of what?

31. What is an OTC drug?

32. What was constructed by Emperor Akbar on the remains of an ancient site known as Badalgarh?

33. Which environment-concerned organization began in 1971 and was then called the 'Don't Make A Wave Committee'?

34. Which planet's most conspicuous feature is the Caloris Basin?

35. What word connects El Dorado, Bullion and California?

36. What is common to Cullinan, Star of the South and Great Mogul?

37. The Empire State building in the US is named after the nickname of which city?

38. Nippon or Nihon is another name for which country?

39. If you consume 0.264 gallons of milk, how many litres would you have consumed?

40. Tides are caused due to the gravitational pull of which celestial body?

41. What is a blood wagon commonly known as?

42. What is a greenhouse made of?

43. Pamulaparti Venkata were the first names of which prime minister of India?

44. If RAM stands for Random Access Memory, what does ROM stand for?
45. What is the Sri Darbar Sahib better known as?
46. Which painter's autobiography is titled *Pandharpur Ka Ek Ladka*?
47. If deforestation means the cutting down of trees, what is the replanting of trees called?
48. In computers, what is a nibble?
49. What were originally sold as waist overalls?
50. In 1864, who became a resident master in Elgin's Weston House Academy in Scotland?

Answers on pages 132–134

WHO AM I?

1.
Clue 1: I was originally named Mortimer.
Clue 2: My first cartoon to be shown to the public was *Steamboat Willie*, in 1928.
Clue 3: 18 November 1928 is recognized as my official birthday.

2.
Clue 1: Born in Lumbini, I was the son of Shuddhodana and Maya.
Clue 2: My meditations under the Bodhi tree helped me attain enlightenment at the age of thirty-five.
Clue 3: I propounded the four Noble Truths and the Eightfold Path which formed the basis of the religion I founded.

3.
Clue 1: I directed my first talkie, *Blackmail*, in 1929.
Clue 2: I was known for making a small appearance in most of the films I directed.
Clue 3: Though acclaimed as the king of suspense and horror, I never won an Oscar for Best Director.

4.

Clue 1: Born in 1879 in Ulm, Germany, I was employed as an examiner at the Swiss patent office in Bern.

Clue 2: I left Germany in the 1930s for the USA in protest against Nazi atrocities.

Clue 3: I won the Nobel Prize in 1921 for my work on the photoelectric effect, though that was not my most famous work.

5.

Clue 1: I am a popular comic-strip character. My dearest friends are Freckles, Pee-Wee and Gloria.

Clue 2: My nasty cousin Reggie Van Dough Jr does his best to upstage me.

Clue 3: I am often called the 'poor little rich boy'.

6.

Clue 1: A famous Indian, I was educated at Harrow School and Cambridge University before studying law.

Clue 2: My books and prison diaries are considered literary classics.

Clue 3: My daughter and my grandson were prime ministers of India.

7.

Clue 1: A great political and military leader, I was born in Prussia in 1815.

Clue 2: I have been credited for leading Germany to its greatest victories as its Chancellor from 1871 to 1890.

Clue 3: You might also know me as 'The Man of Blood and Iron'.

8.

Clue 1: My son Parikshit went on to rule Hastinapur.

Clue 2: My father took revenge for my death by slaying Jayadratha.

Clue 3: I knew how to penetrate the 'Chakravyuha' but was fatally trapped inside.

9.

Clue 1: According to legend, I may be physically distinguished from other men as I do not have a navel.

Clue 2: Another human being was made from one of my ribs.

Clue 3: If I had not eaten the Forbidden Fruit, mankind would not have been created.

10.

Clue 1: Born in Barbados in 1936, I was knighted for my contribution to sport.

Clue 2: A brilliant all-rounder, I share a record with Ravi Shastri.

Clue 3: I scored 8,032 runs in Test cricket and my record of 365 runs in an innings was broken by Brian Lara.

11.

Clue 1: The glory of my reign was described by Chand Bardai in a poem.

Clue 2: I was married to Samyukta, the daughter of Raja Jaichand of Kannauj.

Clue 3: I defeated Muhammad Ghori in the First Battle of Tarain, but was defeated by him a year later.

12.

Clue 1: I was an extremely popular novelist. My first work for children was a collection of poems titled *Child Whispers*.

Clue 2: I also created the Secret Seven series of books.

Clue 3: St Clare's and Malory Towers feature in many of my stories.

13.

Clue 1: I was an outstanding student and joined the Indian Civil Services, but left in 1921 to be part of the Non-Cooperation movement. Because of my activities I was deported to Mandalay.

Clue 2: I founded the Forward Bloc party and was arrested by the British government.

Clue 3: I was the supreme commander of the Indian National Army.

14.

Clue 1: I was born in Sicily between 290–280 BCE and was murdered by a Roman soldier in 212 BCE.

Clue 2: I was supposed to have invented many marvellous machines to fight the Romans and was also considered one of the greatest mathematicians of my time.

Clue 3: You might have heard of me running naked down the streets of Syracuse shouting, 'Eureka, eureka'.

15.

Clue 1: I am a reporter by profession and live at 26 Labrador Road.

Clue 2: My closest friend is a former sea captain who lives in Marlinspike Hall.

Clue 3: Professor Calculus, Jolyon Wagg and Bianca Castafiore are just three of the many characters I meet during my adventures.

16.
Clue 1: I was born in London in 1926. My four children are Charles, Anne, Andrew and Edward.
Clue 2: I married a distant cousin named Philip, and took up my present duties on the death of my father in 1952.
Clue 3: I am the present monarch of the United Kingdom.

17.
Clue 1: Together with my friend Harry East, I was more than a match for Flashman and other bullies.
Clue 2: My school shares its name with a popular sport.
Clue 3: Thomas Hughes created me as an inspiration to schoolboys throughout the world.

18.
Clue 1: I was the first English writer to win the Nobel Prize for Literature.
Clue 2: My well-known poems include 'If' and 'The Ballad of East and West'.
Clue 3: I have created Mowgli, Baloo, Rikki-tikki-tavi and Shere Khan.

19.
Clue 1: I built a laboratory complex in New Jersey and nicknamed it the 'Invention Factory'.
Clue 2: I was named the 'Wizard of Menlo Park'.
Clue 3: I held a world record of 1,093 patents and am also

credited with the invention of the phonograph.

20.
Clue 1: I was the son of King Philip II of Macedon and far outstripped my father's achievements.
Clue 2: My conquests included northwestern India and Egypt.
Clue 3: My encounter with King Porus has become a part of Indian folklore. I died when I was thirty-three.

21.
Clue 1: A famous writer, I was born in 1835 and died in 1910.
Clue 2: My pseudonym was a riverman's term for water 'two fathoms deep'.
Clue 3: Today, the characters Tom Sawyer and Huckleberry Finn, created by me, are known to children throughout the world.

22.
Clue 1: My father was an eminent poet who wrote such classics as *Madhushala*.
Clue 2: I lent my voice to the film *Bhuvan Shome*.
Clue 3: My home, Prateeksha, is a landmark in Mumbai.

23.
Clue 1: I am an eminent Indian. My birthday is celebrated in all educational institutions.
Clue 2: A profound philosopher and a great educationist, I also served as ambassador to the former Soviet Union.
Clue 3: I became the president of India in 1962.

24.

Clue 1: I am a menhir delivery man by profession.

Clue 2: I do not need to drink the magic potion prepared by Getafix the druid, as I fell into a cauldron of potion as a baby.

Clue 3: I often leave my work and join Asterix on his adventures.

25.

Clue 1: I am an Indian movie director.

Clue 2: I directed the film based on Jhumpa Lahiri's novel *The Namesake*.

Clue 3: My production company is called Mirabai Films.

Answers on pages 134–135

LANGUAGE AND LITERATURE

1. Which famous book by Charles Dickens ends with the line: 'God bless us, everyone!'?
2. In the world of literature, how is Rasipuram Krishnaswami Narayan better known?
3. Which novel by Emily Brontë revolves around Heathcliff, Cathy Earnshaw and Edgar Linton?
4. Complete the name of this famous author: Sir Vidiadhar Surajprasad _____
5. Which author's original name was Dhanpat Rai?
6. Fill in the missing word in these lines from a poem by Nissim Ezekiel: 'Thank God the _____ picked on me/ And spared my children.'
7. In which novel does Jean Valjean steal a loaf of bread and is imprisoned?
8. Who was the first American author to submit a typewritten book manuscript?
9. Who created the famous detective Hercule Poirot?
10. Who was lost in a cave with Becky Thatcher?
11. Maid Marian was the companion of which legendary outlaw hero?
12. In the Secret Seven books, what is the name of Peter and Janet's golden spaniel?

13. Which famous novel begins with the words 'Call me Ishmael'?

14. I have a brother named Mycroft. My character is based on the surgeon Dr Joseph Bell. I was created by Sir Arthur Conan Doyle. Who am I?

15. In 'Jack and the Beanstalk', what was Milky White?

16. In which book would you come across the floating island of Laputa and the land of the Houyhnhnms?

17. If you were a cartographer, what would you be studying?

18. In the 1900s, after which famous Russian novelist did Mahatma Gandhi name a colony near Johannesburg?

19. Edward Lear was famous for his five-line humorous poems. What is the correct term for this style of poetry?

20. What would you associate with 'going under the hammer'?

21. What is the plural of Governor-General?

22. In *Twenty Thousand Leagues Under the Sea*, what was the name of the warship in which Captain Nemo sailed?

23. When Jacob and Wilhelm first published them, they were called *Children's and Household Tales*. How are these stories better known today?

24. In Rudyard Kipling's *The Jungle Book*, what kind of a creature was Baloo?

25. In which book would you come across the characters Mercedes and Abbe Faria?

26. What was W.B. Yeats referring to when he said: 'I have carried the manuscripts of these translations around with me for days, reading it in trains or on

the top of buses and in restaurants. I have often had to close it lest some stranger should see how much it moved me.'

27. Who is a couch potato?
28. Which famous author's original name was Charles Lutwidge Dodgson?
29. 'Yours is the Earth and everything that's in it, And—which is more—you'll be a Man, my son!'. These are the last few lines of which poem?
30. Nalappa's Mango Grove and Market Road are located in this fictional town.
31. In the place of which common word would you use an ampersand?
32. Which famous author wrote under the pen name 'Boz'?
33. How many years did Rip Van Winkle sleep?
34. Which was Anna Sewell's only published novel?
35. Which literary character's favourite phrase was 'Off with his head!'?
36. Victor Hugo wrote a novel about a fifteenth-century bell ringer, Quasimodo, who suffered from a physical deformity. Identify the novel.
37. In which popular fictional work would you come across the Cowardly Lion, the Scarecrow and the Tin Woodman?
38. Which word literally means 'empty orchestra' in Japanese?
39. What is defined in the dictionary as 'a report, especially in a newspaper, which gives the news of someone's death and details about their life'?
40. In William Shakespeare's *The Merchant of Venice*,

from whom did Shylock wish to take his pound of flesh?

41. Which word meaning a short official note, memorandum, or voucher, typically recording a sum owed comes from a Hindi word meaning 'note, pass'?

42. Whose autobiography is called *The Fairy Tale of My Life*?

43. Which popular story by Robert Louis Stevenson was originally titled *The Sea Cook*?

44. Which fictional boy fell out of his carriage and was taken by fairies to Never-Never Land?

45. 'Four legs good, two legs bad' is the essence of animalism as described in which book?

46. The phrase red tape signifies official formality and delay. How did this term originate?

47. On her thirteenth birthday, which little girl started writing detailed letters in her diary to an imaginary girlfriend named Kitty?

48. Which story by Louisa May Alcott is about four sisters: Meg, Jo, Beth and Amy?

49. What is a gentleman's agreement?

50. If you had a late morning meal instead of breakfast and lunch, what would you have had?

Answers on pages 135–136

WHAT'S THE QUESTION 2

1. In Roman numerals it is expressed as MXC.
2. It is the common name for the upper entrance to the respiratory system.
3. Pedicure
4. In the Mahabharata, she was the only sister of Duryodhana.
5. Victor, Laverne and Hugo
6. The Holy Grail
7. Khyber Pass
8. In 1962, John Glenn Jr was the first man to do this.
9. There were 150 at this famous circular table.
10. Alopecia is the medical term
11. Isthmus
12. Ornithology
13. Moat
14. Château
15. In India, it is popularly known as imli.
16. Tinker Bell's friend who never grew up
17. Gossima and then ping-pong
18. A comic-strip character whose car is registered with the number 313.
19. Louis and Auguste Lumière

20. The Potala Palace is the winter residence of this religious leader.
21. This fictional character has been played by Sean Connery, David Niven, George Lazenby and Roger Moore on screen.
22. According to the Western zodiac, the name of this constellation means 'goat-horned' in Latin.
23. Mitrabhed and Mitralabh are two of the five chapters of this famous work by Vishnu Sharma.
24. 8,611 metres, making it the second highest in the world.
25. Föhn
26. Filigree
27. Mintonette
28. A naked winged boy with a bow and arrows
29. The Swedish Academy, The Norwegian Committee, The Royal Swedish Academy of Sciences and The Assembly at Karolinska Institutet
30. Gowalia Tank Maidan, Mumbai (now called August Kranti Maidan)
31. Dirham
32. La Marseillaise
33. The Golden Hind
34. Merci beaucoup
35. This theory explains that the universe began with a big explosion.
36. Green Goblin
37. Creutzfeldt-Jakob disease
38. A book called *Our Films, Their Films*
39. A painting called Guernica
40. An Olympic sport involving organized cycle racing and stunt riding on a dirt track

41. With Malice towards One and All
42. This Indian freedom fighter and social reformer transformed Ganesha Chaturthi into a public event in Maharashtra.
43. Haradanahalli
44. Albert Mission School, Vinayak Mudali Street and Lawley Extension
45. The All England Lawn Tennis and Croquet Club
46. He played the role of Dennis the Menace in the 1993 film of the same name.
47. Stretch, Stinkie and Fatso
48. Barkhan
49. Chingachgook and his son Uncas
50. Alpha and Omega

Answers on pages 136–139

FUN FACTS 2

1. Female Anopheles mosquitoes, which carry malaria, kill more than a million people each year.
2. The award given to the director of the Best Feature Film of the official competition at the Cannes Film Festival is known as 'Palme d'Or'.
3. Ada Lovelace, often considered the world's first programmer, was the daughter of the prolific author, Lord Byron.
4. The five-tiered Tugela Falls in South Africa is the second highest waterfall in the world.
5. The first father-son duo to win the Formula One title was Graham and Damon Hill. While Graham won it in 1962 and 1968, Damon won it in 1996.
6. The word 'Yavana', from the Prakrit word 'Yona', is believed to refer originally to Ionian Greeks.
7. In Nepal, jalebi is named 'jeri' after the Mughal emperor Jahangir.
8. Shimla is named after Shyamala Devi, an incarnation of Goddess Kali.
9. There are many plants that produce a rubbery sap, but the rubber tree is the only plant that produces more latex each time it is cut. The wound raises its rate of

photosynthesis, giving each tree a productive life of up to thirty-five years.

10. Pravasi Bharatiya Divas is celebrated every year on 9th January by the Ministry of Overseas Indian Affairs to commemorate Mahatma Gandhi's return to India from South Africa in 1915.

11. The antiseptic and antibiotic properties of clove oil are used in dental medicine.

12. In mythology, Sita is said to be the incarnation of Lakshmi, wife of Lord Vishnu.

HISTORY

1. Which historical place connects Ibrahim Lodi's battle against Babur in 1526, Akbar's victory over Hemu in 1556 and Ahmad Shah Abdali's conflict with the Marathas in 1761?
2. Who invaded Chittorgarh in 1303 because of his passionate desire to abduct Rani Padmini?
3. Which Indian city did Job Charnock 'find' in 1690?
4. Which historically important structure of the Mughals is also known as 'Fort Rouge' or 'Qila-i-Akbari'?
5. In 1910, which Indian prime minister earned an honours degree in natural science from Trinity College, Cambridge?
6. Name the German businessman who saved more than 1,000 Jews from Nazi camps and has been immortalized in an award-winning film?
7. Who was the first Chairman of the Rajya Sabha?
8. In 1930, who started the Vanar Sena, a children's brigade to help freedom fighters?
9. In Indian history, who was the famous wife of Raja Gangadhar Rao?
10. For which famous monument is Ustad Isa credited?

11. Which Indian said, 'Wars cannot be won by bullets, but only by bleeding hearts'?

12. In 1961, which Indian state was liberated from Portuguese rule?

13. 'Karenge ya marenge' (Do or die) was the slogan of which famous movement in India?

14. The historian Bana wrote about which Indian king?

15. Which famous Kushan ruler was referred to as Chia-ni-se-chia in Chinese?

16. Originally known as Khadki or Khidki, which historical town in western India was founded by Malik Ambar in 1610?

17. How was Ram Mohan Roy rewarded by the Mughal emperor of Delhi for going to England and pleading the emperor's case?

18. Which infamous prison would you associate with 14 July 1789?

19. What was Abraham Lincoln referring to when he said, 'If I ever get a chance to hit that thing, I'll hit it hard'?

20. In World War II, what was code-named 'Operation Barbarossa'?

21. Who was the prime minister of the United Kingdom at the time of Queen Elizabeth II's coronation?

22. In which present-day country was the Battle of Waterloo fought?

23. Which famous philosopher was also the tutor of Alexander the Great?

24. By what name is K'ung Fu-tzu better known to the Western world?

25. King Akihito is the ruler of which country?

26. Which city started the first underground metro railway service in 1863?

27. In 79 CE, which natural disaster destroyed the cities of Herculaneum and Pompeii?

28. In 1917, 1944 and 1963, which organization had the unique distinction of being awarded the Nobel Peace Prize?

29. On which famous landmark would you find the words 'Give me your tired, your poor, your huddled masses yearning to breathe free...'?

30. With which unfortunate incident would you associate the warplane Enola Gay?

31. In World War II, what was the US's M-4 General Sherman?

32. In 1939, with which country did Germany sign a Non-Aggression Treaty?

33. Who was the first woman to fly solo across the Atlantic Ocean?

34. Which Japanese military attack on 7 December 1941 was code-named Operation Z?

35. Who introduced the practice of Sijda (prostration) and Paibos (kissing the monarch's feet) in the court as normal forms of salutation to the king?

36. Which famous world leader was accused at the Rivonia Trial?

37. Who was referred to by the title 'Admiral of the Seven Seas'?

38. The *Rigveda Samhita* is divided into ten books. What are the books called?

39. In 1748, who defended Pondicherry against British invasion?

40. Which famous monument is the tomb of Muhammad Adil Shah?

41. In 1922, which incident forced Gandhiji to suspend the Civil Disobedience Movement?

42. The twenty-five windows in which monument symbolize the gemstones found on Earth?

43. In 1325, Prince Jauna became ruler under which name?

44. The Bhavani Talwar belonged to which famous Indian ruler?

45. Whose son was the last Mughal emperor of India?

46. According to legend, which instrument did Nero play while Rome burnt?

47. William and Fanny, the parents of which famous personality, named their child after an Italian town?

48. During World War II, if ll Duce was Benito Mussolini, who was Der Führer?

49. Whose sacred tooth is said to be at Sri Lanka's Temple of the Tooth?

50. In which present-day country was Gautama Buddha born?

Answers on pages 139–140

FOOD

1. What is common to the following: banganapalli, safeda, langra, chausa and malda?
2. What kind of a creature is a Bombay Duck?
3. What is common to cheddar, mozzarella, edam and camembert?
4. Which cuisine, introduced by bawarchis during the reign of the benevolent Nawab Asaf-ud-Daulah over two hundred years ago in Awadh, literally means 'choking off the steam'?
5. Traditionally, which famous sporting event is associated with strawberries and cream?
6. What did the first nizam choose as the official emblem of the Asaf Jahi dynasty?
7. With which Indian community would you associate the dal-meat preparation called 'dhansak'?
8. What is a heavy tool with a rounded end used for crushing and grinding things, typically in a mortar called?
9. The north Indian drink kanji is normally made with a vegetable whose scientific name is *Daucus carota sativis*. How is this vegetable better known?
10. In Kerala, if you are eating karimeen, what would you be eating?

11. Even if they are close to starvation, Inuits never eat penguin eggs. Ever wondered why?

12. Which fruit, rich in papain, an enzyme present in its milky juice, is normally used to make meat tender?

13. What connects Adam and Eve, William Tell and Isaac Newton?

14. Which character by Charles Dickens is famous for his request: 'Please sir, may I have some more'?

15. What is a patty of minced beef, fried or grilled and typically served in a bread roll, and named after Germany's largest port?

16. What is the general name for food such as spaghetti, macaroni and ravioli?

17. Which flavouring agent is called Banira in Japanese?

18. What food has a name which means 'baked twice' in French?

19. An individual banana is referred to by the same name as which part of the human body?

20. What do you call a system of serving when a meal, consisting of several dishes is set out and guests serve themselves?

21. What is common to: tomato, sweet corn, oxtail, bird's nest, chimney and French onion?

22. Corn on the cob is a popular snack in rural America. How do we know it in India?

23. What is the main ingredient in a finger bowl?

24. How do we know the rhizome of the plant *Zingiber officinale*?

25. What is a tandoor oven traditionally made of?

26. In the 1830s, what was marketed in the United States as Dr Miles's compound extract of tomato?

27. Which fruit is sometimes referred to as a love apple?
28. In India, with which food item was Operation Flood associated?
29. If saffron is often referred to as 'Yellow Gold', what is referred to as 'Pink Gold'?
30. By what name is areca nut more popularly known in India?
31. Thomson Seedless, Sonaka, Anab-e-Shahi are the major varieties of which fruit in India?
32. If mutton is associated with sheep, venison is the meat of which animal?
33. Which variety of mango is named after the second governor of sixteenth-century Portuguese India, A de Albuquerque?
34. Which famous cookery show host has written *Khazana of Indian Vegetarian Recipes*?
35. If Christmas is associated with cakes, what food item is Good Friday associated with?
36. In Chinese, what does 'chow mein' literally mean?
37. What is usually added to bread to make it rise?
38. What is the Indian variant of ice cream that is served with faluda?
39. What do you call a south Indian preparation which consists of a crisp rice pancake often with a potato filling served with sambar and coconut chutney?
40. Snoopy and Charlie Brown appear in which comic strip, which has an edible name?
41. Which ice cream sounds as if it has been named after a day of the week?
42. What food makes the cartoon character Popeye strong?

43. What constitutes more than 50 per cent of a dried date, in terms of weight?

44. Which middle eastern dish is a deep-fried ball or patty made from ground chickpeas and/or fava beans?

45. Titled *Kitcha-Yojok*, the first Japanese book on what was written by Buddhist abbot Eisai?

46. If your salt's lacking in I, which mineral would it be lacking in?

47. If you were ordering for food in your hotel room, which two-word department would you ask for?

48. According to popular legend, which famous traveller brought the idea of ice cream to Italy?

49. Which spice consists of the seed of the *Myristica fragrans*, a tropical evergreen tree?

50. What milk-based product is the main ingredient of shrikhand?

Answers on pages 140–142

SPOT THE ANSWER 1

1. What is a pollywog?
   a. A cute golliwog
   b. A green parrot
   c. A tadpole
   d. A resident of Polynesia

2. What was founded at the Gokuldas Tejpal Sanskrit Pathshala?
   a. The Association of Quiz Organizers
   b. The Red Cross in India
   c. The BJP
   d. The Indian National Congress

3. Sansarpur, often known as the Mecca of Hockey, is located in which state of India?
   a. Punjab
   b. West Bengal
   c. Bihar
   d. Maharashtra

4. Which of these monuments is located at Piazza dei Miracoli or Miracles' Square?

a. White House
b. Eiffel Tower
c. Sydney Opera House
d. Leaning Tower of Pisa

5. In the book *The Adventures of Tom Sawyer*, how does the villian, Injun Joe, die?
   a. He is trapped in a cave and dies of starvation.
   b. He drowns in a lake.
   c. A chicken bone gets stuck in his throat.
   d. Tom forces him to swallow a cricket.

6. Who is a cruciverbalist?
   a. An expert at solving crossword puzzles
   b. A person who talks too much
   c. A tightrope walker
   d. A quizmaster's assistant

7. Kiran Bedi was once a champion in which sport?
   a. Kabaddi
   b. Tennis
   c. Karate
   d. Gilli-danda

8. Why was the motto 'Be Prepared' chosen for the Boy Scout Movement?
   a. They were Baden-Powell's favourite two words.
   b. For no reason. Just for kicks.
   c. Based on the initials (BP) of its founder
   d. None of the above

9. How is Princess Manikarnika better known in history?
    a. Steffi Graf (her childhood nickname)
    b. Laika, the first dog in space
    c. Rani Lakshmibai of Jhansi
    d. Nur Jahan

10. Who resides at 221B, Baker Street?
    a. Dennis the Menace
    b. Popeye
    c. Tintin
    d. Sherlock Holmes

11. Why did the British settle in houseboats in Kashmir?
    a. They were barred from buying land.
    b. To protect their daughters from mixing with 'locals'.
    c. The city was too congested and dirty.
    d. To practise their favourite sport: rowing.

12. In 1906, which word was first coined by Maganlal Gandhi in the South African journal *Indian Opinion*?
    a. Ahimsa
    b. Satyagraha
    c. Harijan
    d. Dalit

13. In Japan, who is called 'Maikeru Jakuson'?
    a. The eldest son of the emperor
    b. Michael Jackson
    c. Eldest daughter of the emperor
    d. Mickey Mouse

14. Why is Jaipur called the Pink City?
    a. Because the world's largest pink roses are grown there
    b. It was coloured pink for the Prince of Wales' (King Edward VII) visit in 1876.
    c. It was the third Maharana's daughter's favourite colour.
    d. It was originally painted red. Then it rained!

15. Carl Lewis does not have his 100 metre gold medal from the 1984 Olympics. Why?
    a. He lost it while swimming in the Niagara Falls.
    b. He donated it to UNICEF.
    c. It was robbed from his kit bag.
    d. He put it in his father's coffin.

16. To what did spin bowler Bishan Singh Bedi attribute his strong and supple fingers?
    a. His suffering from polio as a child
    b. His chief coach
    c. Being a champion marble player as a child
    d. Helping his mother make lassi

17. What does an ichthyologist study?
    a. The cause of itch and other skin diseases
    b. Fish
    c. Comics
    d. Eggs of birds

18. What is a croissant?
    a. A crescent-shaped (bread-like) roll made of yeast

    b. A cross-stitch in embroidery
    c. An African spider
    d. The Canadian version of kabaddi

19. Who is a shoeblack?
    a. He removes the make-up of actresses.
    b. The correct term for a person who polishes shoes for a living.
    c. He looks after the slippers/shoes of coal miners.
    d. A person who dyes his hair.

20. Which former state was founded by Dost Mohammed Khan in 1724?
    a. Bhopal
    b. Kolkata
    c. Mumbai
    d. Chandigarh

21. If you were staying at 'The Y', where would you be staying?
    a. The YMCA
    b. The headquarters of Mahesh Yogi
    c. Yamini Krishnamurthy's Dance Academy
    d. In Japan (the Land of the Yen)

22. How did Mount Everest get its name?
    a. After Sir George Everest, the then Surveyor General of India
    b. After the Greek god of mountains
    c. Edmund Hillary's childhood nickname was 'Everest'
    d. After Lord John Henry Everest, Viceroy of Nepal

23. What happens at an 'abattoir'?
    a. Animals are slaughtered.
    b. Hindi film stuntmen receive first aid.
    c. Hens lay artificial eggs.
    d. People play video games.

24. What did Pingali Venkaiah design, which was adopted by India's Constituent Assembly on 22 July 1947?
    a. The Indian National Flag
    b. Madhuri Dixit's costumes in *Khalnayak*
    c. The Rashtrapati Bhavan
    d. The AIR logo

25. On what grounds was Surendranath Banerjee's admission to the Indian Civil Service (now IAS) rejected?
    a. He misrepresented his age.
    b. His IQ was below fifty-five.
    c. He wrote 'surrender not' instead of Surendranath.
    d. Because only women were allowed in the ICS

26. Why was champion swimmer Dawn Fraser banned from competitions for many years?
    a. She stole the Japanese royal flag at the Tokyo Olympics.
    b. She tested positive for drugs.
    c. She was a 'man' participating as a woman.
    d. She burnt a kimono in public.

27. What is a leveret?
    a. A machine to lift heavy weight

    b. The young of a hare
    c. A remote control
    d. A leopard den

28. Euphemistically, what is a 'marble orchard'?
    a. A shop which sells coloured playing marbles
    b. A graveyard, because of the marble tombstones
    c. A toilet decorated with glazed tiles
    d. A garden where apples are grown

29. In India, if the Green Revolution referred to grains, and the White Revolution to milk, what did the Blue Revolution refer to?
    a. Tourism
    b. Production of fish
    c. Strawberries
    d. Holi played every year by Bollywood stars

30. What was the Bombay Pentangular?
    a. The five-storied Kapoor home
    b. A pre-Independence cricket tournament
    c. The five top film studios before Independence
    d. The first train to run between Bombay and Surat

31. Arabica and Robusta are two main varieties of what?
    a. Horse
    b. Coffee
    c. Biryani
    d. Silk

32. In swimming in the US, other than holding aloft a sign, how is the last lap of a race signalled?

a. By ringing a bell
b. By screaming 'Go man, go'
c. By firing a gun
d. There is no signal!

33. What is fly ash?
   a. Mosquitoes killed by repellents
   b. Aishwarya Rai's private helicopter
   c. Small dark flecks produced by the burning of powdered coal or other materials
   d. Smoke

34. Who founded the 'Heal the World Foundation', for the safety, health and development of children?
   a. Hillary Clinton
   b. Laloo Prasad Yadav
   c. Mother Teresa
   d. Michael Jackson

35. Which famous Indian's ashes were lying in the main branch of the State Bank of India in Cuttack since 1950?
   a. Dr S. Radhakrishnan
   b. Sarojini Naidu
   c. K.L. Saigal
   d. Mahatma Gandhi

36. The Incas had no form of writing, instead, they had relay runners conveying messages by carrying what they called 'quipus'. What were quipus?
   a. Double-sided mirrors

    b. Knotted designs of human hair
    c. Messages in bottles
    d. Colour-coded arrangements of knotted threads

37. Which king called himself Devanampiya Piyadasi or beloved of the gods and handsome in looks?
    a. Ashoka
    b. Prithviraj Chauhan
    c. Maharana Pratap
    d. Harshavardhana

38. Of what are A4 and B5 sizes?
    a. Diamond
    b. Briefs and vests
    c. CD-Roms
    d. Paper

39. What do you call a Western film made cheaply in Europe by an Italian director?
    a. Pizza Westerns
    b. Masala Westerns
    c. Macaroni Westerns
    d. Spaghetti Westerns

40. Why is House 54 on University Avenue, in Rangoon, a big tourist attraction?
    a. It was the house where Aung San Suu Kyi was kept under house arrest.
    b. The site of the world's largest pagoda
    c. Lord Mountbatten's grave
    d. Tiananmen Square memorial

41. The Chinese expression Kung Hei Fat Choi, means...
    a. Have a prosperous and happy new year
    b. Good luck for the quiz
    c. Happy birthday
    d. I love you

42. In whose honour was 29 August chosen as National Sports Day in India?
    a. Milkha Singh's birthday
    b. Dhyan Chand's birthday
    c. Sunil Gavaskar's birthday
    d. India's win in the 1983 Cricket World Cup

43. Some cough mixtures have the word 'linctus' in them, what is the origin of the term?
    a. Contains lime
    b. To be licked
    c. Contains linoleum
    d. Heals tonsilitis

44. What is common to owls, aardvark, kiwi and bats?
    a. They all sleep on their backs.
    b. They generally hunt at night.
    c. They were all used as Olympic mascots.
    d. They are only found in New Zealand.

45. What would a Chinese individual do with a wok?
    a. Burst it. (Chinese cracker)
    b. Eat it. (Dumpling)
    c. Sleep in it. (Hammock)
    d. Cook in it. (Chinese cooking vessel)

46. How did Ranjit Singh lose one of his eyes?
    a. Injury while playing polo
    b. Born with one eye
    c. Due to smallpox
    d. His pet vulture injured him.

47. Prince Philip is the President Emeritus of which of these organizations?
    a. World Wildlife Fund
    b. World Wrestling Federation
    c. World Whale Foundation
    d. Welsh Women's Forum

48. Which collection of stories is also called *Alf laylah wa laylah*?
    a. *Arabian Nights*
    b. *Jataka Tales*
    c. *Panchatantra*
    d. *Hitopadesha*

49. Who was the king of Japan during World War II?
    a. Ajinomoto
    b. Hirohito
    c. Akihito
    d. Yokozuna

50. The dog that would eventually evolve into Mickey Mouse's dog Pluto made his debut in *The Chain Gang* as a...
    a. Dachshund
    b. Mixed breed

c. Bloodhound
d. King Charles VI Spaniel

Answers on pages 142–145

WHAT'S THE QUESTION 3

1. Schiphol Airport
2. It comprised one big Oscar and seven little ones.
3. Trinity and Cyclops
4. Scuffing (in cricket)
5. He wrote *Our Trees Still Grow in Dehra*
6. Nadir Shah gave its name
7. *Moonwalk* (book)
8. Changi Airport
9. Kyats
10. William the Conqueror defeated King Harold II of England
11. LaGuardia Airport
12. Britain, France, Sardinia and Turkey defeated Russia in 1853–1856
13. *Pride and Prejudice* is one of her most famous novels.
14. Ringgit
15. Killing the Nemean lion and killing the Lernaean Hydra
16. They were a race of one-eyed giants; one of them was Polyphemus.
17. He married Dimple Kapadia in 1973.

18. In Asterix comics, after drinking it, the drinker's strength increases.
19. Ophiuchus
20. Guilder
21. This war ended in 1918.
22. From 1979 onwards, they are named alphabetically, alternating between male and female names.
23. *Goal*
24. Bram Stoker
25. UN Day
26. The flag of Mexico
27. Spirit of St Louis
28. It is a word puzzle with a grid of squares and blanks.
29. 11 Downing Street
30. Nephrons are the functional units of this organ.
31. It was Ian Fleming's only children's story.
32. Jacob Schick
33. It is a deadly disease caused by a bacteria, *Yersinia pestis.*
34. Kill Devil Hills
35. The Kauravas and Pandavas fought their great war here.
36. This fish is also known as 'caribe'.
37. His name is Kvack.
38. In 1862, he proposed the formation of voluntary relief societies in his book *A Memory of Solferino.*
39. He wrote *Indica.*
40. Emperor, Gentoo, Galapagos
41. Seville, Jaffa and Sunkist
42. It is the hardest tissue of the body.
43. Barbara Millicent Roberts

44. He directed *Hazaar Chaurasi Ki Maa.*
45. This space term comes from the Latin words meaning 'space' and 'sailor'.
46. Filofax
47. It is a piece of metal or plastic used to help the foot into the shoe.
48. This portable stereo cassette player with headphones was invented in 1979.
49. It is called 'loo' in north India.
50. This unit of measurement comes from 'binary' and 'digit'.

Answers on pages 145–147

FUN FACTS 3

1. The loudest animals on land are howler monkeys, who can be heard three miles away.
2. Karan Johar won the Filmfare Award for Best Director for *My Name is Khan* in 2011, which was twelve years after he had won it for *Kuch Kuch Hota Hai*.
3. Geoffrey Chaucer was the first poet to be buried in Westminster Abbey, in what is known as the 'Poets' Corner'.
4. Angel Falls, the highest waterfall in the world, drops off a flat-topped plateau called 'Devil's Mountain'.
5. The first cricketer to hit 100 sixes in Test cricket was Adam Gilchrist.
6. The first Hindu expert in Algebra was Aryabhatta I. About thirty-three of his slokas form a section of the astronomical work *Aryabhatiya*.
7. Goat is the world's most consumed meat.
8. In 2007, at the age of thirty-six, Bobby Jindal created history by becoming the first-ever Indian American to be elected governor of a US state.
9. Kashmiris often carry an earthen pot known as the kangri, inside the Kashmiri cloak, the pheran, to keep themselves warm.

10. Qawwali is said to have been derived from the devotional songs originally sung by the Sufi saints at Sufi shrines or dargahs throughout South Asia.
11. In Hindu mythology, Jarasandha was created by joining two halves of a child, by a giantess named Jara.
12. The name coriander comes from a Greek word meaning 'bug', referring to the 'buggy' or offensive smell it has when unripe.

SCIENCE

1. If they were not in your geometry book, where would you find your radius and ulna?
2. Find the odd one out: bronze, zinc, brass, pewter.
3. Liquefied Petroleum Gas (LPG) is chemically odourless. Yet whenever this cooking gas leaks, we can smell it. Why?
4. Who was the first woman to win a Nobel Prize?
5. By what name is acetylsalicylic acid better known?
6. What useful mathematical tool is John Napier's most famous invention?
7. Which gas protects the Earth from harmful ultraviolet rays?
8. Find the odd one out: Pascal, Newton, Basic, Cobol and Algol.
9. Adams, Leverrier, Galle and Lassell are some of the rings of which planet?
10. Which is the closest star to the Earth?
11. What is common to the following terms: beam, arch, cantilever and suspension?
12. In a rainbow, which colour comes between blue and yellow?
13. More than 95 per cent of human deaths caused by

rabies occur in Asia and which other continent?

14. In computer jargon, what does GIGO stand for?

15. Patients belonging to which blood group are said to be 'universal receivers'?

16. By subtracting 32, dividing by 9 and multiplying by 5, what conversion can be made?

17. Which element's chemical symbol Au derives from the Latin aurum, for Aurora the goddess of dawn?

18. What is common to simple, greenstick, Pott's or impacted?

19. Alexander Graham Bell's notebook entry of 10 March 1876 describes the first successful experiment with which instrument?

20. Fill in the blank: the wheel and axle, the lever, the ramp, the screw and the pulley are all_____ machines.

21. If your friends kept away from you because your axilla was smelling, which part of the body would the axilla be?

22. Collectively, how many moons do the planets Mercury and Venus have?

23. In 1806, which typist's time saver was patented by Ralph Wedgwood?

24. According to Newton's Third Law of Motion, what is there to every action?

25. Which natural process gets its name from the Greek words meaning 'light' and 'together'?

26. Think logically! Which planet was the first to be explored by man?

27. Which two scientists' laboratory notebooks were checked for radiation before being auctioned in 1984?

28. What would a graphologist study?
29. Which part of the body is affected by glaucoma?
30. Why is tungsten used in the electric bulb?
31. What does a car's radiator do?
32. If you had excess bilirubin in your bloodstream, what would you be suffering from?
33. Which word connects the repetition of sound caused by the reflection of sound waves and a code word representing the letter E, used in radio communication?
34. If a small circle has 360 degrees, how many degrees does a big circle have?
35. With which organ of the human body would you associate the word 'renal'?
36. In the binary system, which two digits represent all numbers?
37. What kind of magnet can be switched on and off?
38. Encephalitis is a disease that affects the brain. Which part of your body is affected when you have hepatitis?
39. Which is the odd one out and why: ringworm, hookworm, tapeworm and roundworm?
40. Bronze is an alloy traditionally composed of copper and_____
41. Which household implement, invented by Hubert Cecil Booth, was originally called the Puffing Billy?
42. Despite high temperatures, why do the filaments of light bulbs not burn?
43. Which is the hardest naturally occurring substance known?
44. Which rodent gives its name to a device attached to a computer?

45. If your larynx was removed, what handicap would you suffer from?
46. Which is the only planet not to be named after Greek and Roman gods and goddesses?
47. What is the correct geometric name of an equilateral parallelogram?
48. Which organ in the human body is the word 'pulmonary' connected with?
49. What important part did James Phipps play in the history of medicine?
50. In 1980, the World Health Organization declared the world free of which disease?

Answers on pages 147–149

WILDLIFE

1. The brown bear and the Himalayan bear are both found in India. In which country would you find a koala bear in the wild?
2. Which animal has been on the logo of World Wide Fund for Nature (WWF) since 1961?
3. Which creature is considered the most intelligent of all invertebrates?
4. Which North American animal is referred to as the 'Silvertip Bear' because the tips of the hair on its body is silver-coloured?
5. Only one forest is the home of the Asiatic lion. Name it.
6. What was the name of the lioness in *Born Free*?
7. The Indian name of this snake is ajgar. What is its English name?
8. Which carnivorous mammal found in the Himalayan range is also called the ounce?
9. In a colony of bees, what are male bees called?
10. Which is the only member of the cat family to live in groups called prides?
11. The height of which animal is measured in 'hands'?
12. Which national park has the unique distinction of

harbouring last of the world's population of highly endangered hard ground barasingha?

13. What are brood parasites?

14. A camel's stomach is divided into how many chambers?

15. How many miles can a full-grown ostrich fly?

16. What is North America's largest rodent?

17. In Spanish it means 'little fly'. How do we know this biting insect?

18. How many fish would you have if you had one cod, three jellyfish and four crayfish?

19. Which bird has the largest known wingspan of any living bird?

20. Which present-day animal did the prehistoric mammoth closely represent?

21. Which five-letter word is used for an American buffalo?

22. Which is the only snake to build a nest?

23. The elephant's tusk is made of ivory. What is a rhinoceros' horn made of?

24. What are you most likely to find inside a 'mermaid's purse'?

25. Siberian, Sumatran and Bengal are species of which animal?

26. The largest variety of which creature is the Komodo Dragon?

27. A tigon is an offspring of a tiger and a lioness. What do you call the offspring of a lion and a tigress?

28. The name of which creature comes from the Greek words meaning 'terrible lizard'?

29. The duck-billed platypus and the echidna or spiny

anteater are the only two mammals to do what?

30. Which is the only floating national park in the world?

31. Which reptile in India gets its name from an Indian water pot?

32. What don't Manx cats and humans have, that monkeys and other cats do?

33. Barking, swamp, musk and rein are all types of which animal?

34. Which animal's name translates from Scandinavian as 'horse whale'?

35. Elephant, crabeater, harp and leopard are all species of which creature?

36. What is common to Arctic, Red, Fennec and Indian?

37. Siamese, Persian, Caffre and Sphynx are all types of which animal?

38. A rabbit's tail is called a scut. What is a fox's tail called?

39. Name the largest species of rat found in India. (Hint: In Telugu, it is called pandi-kokku.)

40. The name of which animal comes from a Native American word meaning 'he who kills with one leap'?

41. It is one of the largest Indian antelopes. The male of the species has a smooth bluish-grey coat and is also called 'blue bull'. How is it commonly known in India?

42. A badger's burrow is called a sett. What do you call a hare's lair?

43. In which state is the Pench National Park located?

44. Which is the largest animal known to have ever lived on Earth?

45. Black Widow is a species of which creature?

46. The male of which bird, with the scientific name *Luscinia megarhynchos*, mostly sings at night?
47. Name the most well-known extinct flightless bird of Mauritius.
48. Name the odd one out of the following animals and state why: opossum, koala, wombat, giant panda and wallaby.
49. In Hindi, it is called bhaloo. What is it called in English?
50. Where on a butterfly's body is its sense of taste located?

Answers on pages 149–151

MIXED BAG 2

1. What appears over crossed bones on the danger sign?
2. What is common to Paul McCartney, Jimmy Connors, George Bush and Leonardo da Vinci?
3. In the field of education, what is common to Kanpur, Kharagpur, Mumbai, Delhi and Chennai?
4. Which is the only complete book authored by the Nazi leader Adolf Hitler?
5. Who was awarded the Nobel Prize 'because of his profoundly sensitive, fresh and beautiful verse, by which, with consummate skill, he has made his poetic thought, expressed in his own English words, a part of the literature of the West'?
6. What is the national television network of Sri Lanka called?
7. Which shehnai player was born on 21 March 1916 in Bihar?
8. Which famous South African leader is popularly known as Madiba?
9. On a Scrabble board, the score for an entire word is tripled when one of its letters is placed on a square of which colour?

10. Where would you find the following: down, across, clues and squares?

11. United States Patent No. 174465, issued in 1876, and recognized as the 'most valuable patent' was for what?

12. What pledge would you find on an Indian currency note?

13. I am a nine-letter word. My first letter is the Roman letter for 100. The next three are a zodiac sign and the last two are the name of the Egyptian Sun God. Who am I?

14. With which musical instrument would you associate maestro Vilayat Khan?

15. Which author was known by the pseudonym Saki?

16. On 16 April 1853, the first train on Indian soil ran between Thane and which city?

17. Who is the first Indian woman to scale the summit of Mount Everest?

18. Veer Savarkar and Vinoba Bhave share which first name?

19. Which English author stated that one of her goals in writing was 'to induce kindness, sympathy, and an understanding treatment of horses'?

20. Which Mughal emperor gave Allahabad its present name?

21. Who did Mahatma Gandhi call the 'Prince among Patriots'?

22. The Bharat Ratna award is designed in the shape of which leaf?

23. *Oryza sativa* is the scientific name of which food grain?

24. Which political leader, born in Braunau am Inn, wanted to buy Dhyan Chand's hockey stick?

25. What is the surname of the Maratha king Shivaji?
26. Which monument was formerly known as the Black Pagoda?
27. Which prime minister of Pakistan did Khwaja Nazimuddin succeed?
28. Kargil is in which Lok Sabha constituency?
29. Which portfolio did Indira Gandhi hold in the government of Lal Bahadur Shastri?
30. Whom did C.V. Raman refer to as the modern equivalent of Leonardo da Vinci?
31. Who is the author of *Ramcharitmanas*?
32. Which brother of Kishore Kumar worked as a lab assistant in Bombay Talkies?
33. Who is the only US president to be awarded the Pulitzer Prize?
34. The playing time of the full version of the Indian National Anthem is approximately how many seconds?
35. Whose autobiography is titled *The Story of My Experiments with Truth*?
36. Loggerhead, leatherback and hawksbill are species of which reptile?
37. The name of which Union Territory means 'hundred thousand islands' in Sanskrit?
38. Which month in the Gregorian calendar is named after Julius Caesar?
39. Which famous leader was Vijaya Lakshmi Pandit's brother?
40. Which lake in India shares its name with the Hindi name of pulses?
41. A high plateau named Lakshmi Planum is located on which planet?

42. The Euro symbol is inspired by which Greek letter?
43. In terms of transport, what connects an autorickshaw and a tricycle?
44. What was the code name of the Indian operation in the Kargil war?
45. Who has been India's longest-serving prime minister?
46. Which Mughal emperor was born at Umarkot in 1542?
47. Who has written the national anthem of Bangladesh?
48. 'The Parish Boy's Progress' is the subtitle of which novel by Charles Dickens?
49. Who set up a dance school called Nrityagram near Bangalore?
50. In which city is the Salar Jung Museum located?

Answers on pages 151–152

SPORTS

1. Nadia Comaneci was the first woman to obtain a perfect 10 in Olympic gymnastics. Who was the first man?
2. Which famous Brazilian died in Imola at the San Marino Grand Prix in 1994?
3. Which word was included in the Oxford English Dictionary as a result of a sporting incident in 1932–33?
4. In chess, to which organization does 'Sicilian Defence' owe its name?
5. Which was the first Asian non-capital city to host the Asian Games?
6. Who was the first athletics coach to win the Dronacharya Award?
7. In 1985, who became the first unseeded player to win the Wimbledon Men's Singles tournament?
8. Which famous Hungarian footballer was known as 'The Galloping Major'?
9. *Back to the Mark* is the autobiography of which former fast bowler?
10. If someone participates in Le Mans, then in which sport is he an expert?

11. In athletics, over how many days is the decathlon spread?

12. The Spanish footballer Emilio Butragueno was nicknamed after which bird?

13. In *Alice's Adventures in Wonderland*, which game was played by the Queen of Hearts using hedgehogs as balls?

14. In Indian football if the 'Red and Gold' is up against the 'Maroon and Green', then which two teams are playing?

15. Who is the first Indian to claim a hat-trick in an ODI match?

16. The first Indian chess Grandmaster was Vishwanathan Anand. Who is the second?

17. The three Ws of West Indian cricket (Weekes, Worrell and Walcott) all hailed from which island?

18. Which sport would you be playing if you represented your school in Subroto Mukherjee Cup?

19. Which sportsman was once nicknamed 'The Louisville Lip' because of the way he used to boast before a contest?

20. In which sport does the Boston Celtics compete against the Denver Nuggets?

21. Which former cricketer was nicknamed 'Big C' or 'Hubert'?

22. Bobby Riggs was fifty-five when he lost a challenge match against which woman tennis star?

23. What is common to the following: George Hackenschmidt, the Great Gama, Ed Lewis and Frank Gotch?

24. Which Indian emulated Bob Massie's feat of sixteen wickets on Test debut?

25. Who was the first Indian to captain the Oxford University cricket team?
26. Who succeeded Bobby Fischer as World Chess Champion in 1975?
27. The contingent of which country marches last in the Olympic march past?
28. In which athletic event did Dick Fosbury invent a new technique and by employing it won an Olympic gold medal in 1968?
29. *With Time to Spare* is one of the autobiographies of which English left-handed batsman?
30. In the 1992 Cricket World Cup, who or what was Daddles?
31. If 'Big Bird' is the nickname for cricketer Joel Garner, then which footballer was nicknamed the 'Little Bird'?
32. What reason did King Edward III give for banning football in 1365?
33. If you are fielding at the 'long stop' position in cricket, where would you be positioned?
34. What are the two basic categories in diving events at the Olympic games?
35. Which Indian bowler's memoir is titled *One More Over*?
36. The football team of which country was once referred to as the 'Magical Magyars'?
37. Which ball game was invented by James Naismith in 1891, to help his students keep fit during winter?
38. Which stadium hosted the Football World Cup finals of both 1986 and 1970?
39. What is the colour at the centre of an archery target?
40. Which is the only chess piece that cannot move to

a black square if it had started the game in a white square?

41. If in swimming you might use the dolphin kick, in which sport would you use the banana and the scissors kick?

42. Which game can be played on three different mounts: horse, cycle and elephant?

43. Which team has reached the Cricket World Cup final three times but failed to win on any occasion?

44. What was unique about the 1994 FIFA World Cup preliminary round match between USA and Switzerland?

45. Ivan Lendl and Martina Navratilova represented USA in international competitions later in their careers. Which country did they originally belong to by birth?

46. On 11 January 1959, how did Hanif Mohammed get out at 499 attempting his 500th run?

47. In 1977, Pelé played his last competitive match involving Santos and New York Cosmos. For which team did he play in that match?

48. Which cricketer's autobiography is titled *Beyond 10,000, My Life Story*?

49. Grandmaster is the highest classification for a chess player. What is the classification immediately below it?

50. Which German football player is credited with inventing the 'attacking sweeper' position?

Answers on pages 152–154

FUN FACTS 4

1. A single sea wasp (a kind of jellyfish with sixty tentacles) has enough venom to kill sixty people.
2. Manna Dey has recorded more than 3,500 songs. The Government of India honoured him with the Padma Shri in 1971, the Padma Bhushan in 2005 and the Dadasaheb Phalke Award in 2007.
3. The classic novel *Gone With the Wind* was originally titled *Baa! Baa! Black Sheep.*
4. The Galápagos Islands, discovered by the Spanish in 1535, were named after the giant land tortoises found there. (Galápagos means 'tortoises' in Spanish).
5. Traditionally, Greece leads the Parade of Nations in any Olympics and the host comes in last. In 2004, when Greece hosted it, they sent in their flag first and the athletes last.
6. Russia, the world's largest country, covers nearly twice the territory of Canada, the second largest country.
7. Popcorn in popped form comes in two basic shapes: snowflake and mushroom.
8. The flag of Cambodia, which carries an image of the Angkor Wat, is the only national flag in the world to incorporate an actual building in its design.

9. Daphne Blake, in the Scooby-Doo cartoon series, comes from a wealthy family. Her father's money provided the gang with the Mystery Machine, a 1960s-era hippie van.

10. Pallivasal, located about 8 km from Munnar, is the venue of the first hydroelectric project in Kerala.

11. According to legend, Brahma gifted Harishchandra II a palace which produced everything desired by its owner.

12. In Indian cooking, chhaunk is another word for vaghar or tadka.

SPOT THE ANSWER 2

1. After which freedom fighter is the Marine National Park in Andaman named?
    a. Subhas Chandra Bose
    b. Bhagat Singh
    c. Rani of Jhansi
    d. Mahatma Gandhi

2. The Danjon scale, ranging from L=0 (meaning very dark) to L=4 (meaning very bright copper red to orange), measures the brightness of which phenomenon?
    a. Lunar eclipse
    b. Aurora Borealis
    c. Rainbow
    d. Earthquake

3. In Japan, what would you do with a kimono?
    a. Wear it.
    b. Eat it.
    c. Write with it.
    d. Sleep on it.

4. Noshak is the highest point of which country?
    a. Pakistan
    b. China
    c. Afghanistan
    d. Bangladesh

5. How did espresso coffee get its name?
    a. A variation of the word 'express'
    b. From the word 'espressino', meaning cold coffee
    c. From the magical words 'Hey presto'
    d. From the Italian word for 'pressed out'

6. With reference to the World Wide Web, what does the term 'hit rate' refer to?
    a. Cricket scores on the net
    b. Being hit by a virus
    c. The number of visitors to a website
    d. The number of files downloaded illegally

7. In Hindi films, Begum Mumtaz Jehan Dehlavi was the original name of which actress?
    a. Madhubala
    b. Meena Kumari
    c. Asha Parekh
    d. Waheeda Rahman

8. Which country once used money shaped like knives?
    a. Egypt
    b. Korea
    c. China
    d. Russia

9. Why do bees perform a complicated movement called the 'waggle dance'?
   a. To teach young bees to fly
   b. To tell other bees where to find food
   c. To warn bees from other hives
   d. To fluff out leg hairs to collect pollen

10. Who sang 'The Song for Peace' minutes before he was assassinated?
   a. John F. Kennedy
   b. Abraham Lincoln
   c. Yitzhak Rabin
   d. Mahatma Gandhi

11. What is a plectrum used for?
   a. To strum a stringed instrument
   b. To break light into various colours
   c. To safeguard electrical appliances
   d. To stand on when making a speech

12. Which cartoon character is called 'Skipper Skræk' in Denmark?
   a. Tintin
   b. Asterix
   c. Popeye
   d. Shaggy

13. In medieval times, a knight threw down a gauntlet to challenge someone to a duel. Which part of his attire did a gauntlet refer to?
   a. The plume from his helmet
   b. His gloves

   c. His broadsword
   d. His signet ring

14. Fidel Castro ordered the seizure of all sets of which game in Cuba?
   a. Snakes and ladders
   b. Scrabble
   c. Chess
   d. Monopoly

15. The word 'solstice' comes from the Latin phrase meaning...
   a. A salt cellar
   b. A five-pointed star
   c. Sunstroke
   d. Sun stands still

16. The word simian is used to describe what?
   a. Sheep
   b. Snakes
   c. Monkeys
   d. Foxes

17. Hidrosis is the medical term for...
   a. Water in the brain
   b. Death due to drowning
   c. A running nose
   d. Perspiration

18. Which soccer star is nicknamed 'Dennis the Menace'?
   a. Diego Maradona
   b. Eric Cantona

    c.   Dennis Bergkamp
    d.   George Weah

19. How is nyctalopia better known?
    a.   Blindness
    b.   Conjunctivitis
    c.   Short sightedness
    d.   Night blindness

20. What would the term 'Round Robin' best describe?
    a.   A bird's nest
    b.   A tournament in which competitors play in turn against each other
    c.   One of Robin Hood's followers
    d.   A steamed pudding

21. The spacecraft Clementine discovered which of these, that increases the chances that humans may some day live on the moon?
    a.   A golf ball
    b.   A pond of frozen ice in a crater
    c.   Microscopic single-celled organisms
    d.   Traces of oxygen in the moon's atmosphere

22. Which of the seven ancient wonders of the world can still be seen today?
    a.   Pyramids of Giza
    b.   Hanging Gardens of Babylon
    c.   Pharos of Alexandria
    d.   The Colossus of Rhodes

23. Who wrote *Man-Eaters of Kumaon*?
    a. Jim Corbett
    b. Rohinton Mistry
    c. Ruskin Bond
    d. Mulk Raj Anand

24. On what occasion did Sarojini Naidu write to Jawaharlal Nehru: 'Love to all and a kiss to the new soul of India'?
    a. When India achieved independence
    b. On the birth of Indira Gandhi
    c. At the start of the Quit India Movement
    d. After he was sworn in as prime minister

25. In *Gulliver's Travels*, what caused the war between Lilliput and its neighbour?
    a. Whether to break the broad or narrow end of an egg
    b. The gold in Gulliver's ship
    c. A land dispute
    d. Whether to eat soup or drink soup

26. The Tibetans call it Chomolungma, meaning 'Goddess Mother of the World'. What is its English name?
    a. Yak
    b. Mount Everest
    c. Mother Earth
    d. Godwin-Austen or K2

27. Her native name was Ma Tint Tint. She later became Usha. Who was she?
    a. P.T. Usha

b. India's former first lady Usha Narayanan

c. Usha Mangeshkar

d. Usha Uthup

28. Where might you see Nishi warriors with hornbill caps and knives in monkey-skin scabbards?

a. Russia

b. Madhya Pradesh

c. Japan

d. Arunachal Pradesh

29. In 1524, which famous explorer was buried in St Francis Church, Fort Kochi?

a. Ferdinand Magellan

b. Christopher Columbus

c. Amerigo Vespucci

d. Vasco da Gama

30. Traditionally, who uses a gold broom and acts as 'sweeper to the gods' at the Puri Rath Yatra?

a. The head priest

b. The raja of Puri

c. The oldest pilgrim

d. The chief minister of Odisha

31. What is the difference between kajal and kohl?

a. Kajal is for the eyelashes while kohl is for the eyebrows.

b. Kajal is for adults, kohl is for children.

c. There is no difference.

d. Kajal is made from carbon, while kohl is herbal.

32. According to Aristotle, what is the best provision for old age?
    a. Money
    b. Education
    c. Children
    d. A bungalow

33. Which phrase is used to describe a prime minister's inner cabinet or most trusted members?
    a. Bedroom cabinet
    b. Shadow cabinet
    c. Godrej kitchen
    d. Kitchen cabinet

34. Which children's novel by Dodie Smith is also a Walt Disney film?
    a. *The Little Mermaid*
    b. *The Lion King*
    c. *101 Dalmatians*
    d. *Pocahontas*

35. How is Kongzi better known to us?
    a. Confucius
    b. Dalai Lama
    c. Bruce Lee
    d. Osho Rajneesh

36. Which system of medical practice is based on 'let like cure like'?
    a. Allopathy
    b. Acupuncture

    c. Ayurveda

    d. Homeopathy

37. What would you do with a tom yum?
    a. Play with it. It is a yo-yo.
    b. Climb it. It is the highest mountain in China.
    c. Sing it. It is the Burmese national anthem.
    d. Eat it. It is a Thai soup.

38. Which tree did Tipu Sultan declare as a royal tree and monopolized its trade in 1792?
    a. Banyan
    b. Mango
    c. Sandalwood
    d. Mahogany

39. What is vellum, used for writing or printing on, made from?
    a. Wood from the banyan tree
    b. Animal skins
    c. Wood from the eucalyptus tree
    d. Goat's intestines

40. In computer terminology, what is 'wetware'?
    a. The human brain
    b. A freshly printed page
    c. The best swimsuit catalogue on the Internet
    d. An ink cartridge for a bubble jet printer

41. Which of these was invented first?
    a. Spectacles
    b. Radio

  c. Television sets
  d. Atom bomb

42. In which novel by Charles Dickens would you meet
  Agnes Wickfield, James Steerforth and Clara Peggotty?
  a. *A Christmas Carol*
  b. *Oliver Twist*
  c. *David Copperfield*
  d. *Dombey and Son*

43. How many milligrams make a kilogram?
  a. One thousand
  b. Ten thousand
  c. One million
  d. Ten million

44. With which sport would you associate the jumping
  style called Fosbury Flop?
  a. Long jump
  b. High jump
  c. Pole vault
  d. Triple jump

45. Who among these was the son of a Pandava?
  a. Jatasura
  b. Mahishasura
  c. Ravana
  d. Ghatotkacha

46. The South China Sea divides which country into two
  parts?
  a. Malaysia

b. Brunei

c. Cambodia

d. Turkey

47. In which novel by Charles Dickens was the main character haunted by three spirits who took him to the past, present and future?

   a. *A Christmas Carol*

   b. *Oliver Twist*

   c. *David Copperfield*

   d. *The Pickwick Papers*

48. The flightless bird rhea is native to which continent?

   a. Africa

   b. South America

   c. Australia

   d. Asia

49. Which is the human body's biggest consumer of oxygen and the first organ to suffer if there is a shortage?

   a. Brain

   b. Kidney

   c. Heart

   d. Liver

50. In 1813–14, Ranjit Singh, the king of Punjab, brought what back to India?

   a. Peacock Throne

   b. Koh-i-noor diamond

   c. His title

   d. Akbar's sword

Answers on pages 154–156

1. Alexander Selkirk, a Scottish sailor, provided the inspiration for the story.
2. The group of twelve who decide if a person is guilty or innocent.
3. In the Mahabharata, she was Abhimanyu's mother.
4. It is the only country to have a non-rectangular or square flag.
5. The fattest of Robin Hood's merry men.
6. A game in which players buy and sell houses and hotels.
7. Mount Pidurutalagala is the highest point of this country.
8. This horizontal bone connects the shoulder blade and the sternum.
9. This machine's name comes from Latin, meaning 'to make similar'.
10. This Mughal emperor, the son of Shah Jahan, called himself Alamgir (World Conqueror).
11. This part of a radio is also called an aerial.
12. A mollusc with three hearts and eight arms
13. Elephants use this for smelling, breathing, trumpeting, drinking and also to grab things.
14. In chess notation, this piece is designated as N.

15. Approximately, 78 per cent nitrogen, 21 per cent oxygen and 1 per cent other gases
16. The letters Q, U, X, Y and Z are never used in its naming by the World Meteorological Organization.
17. This zone of treeless, level or rolling ground north of the Arctic Circle or above the timberline on high mountains covers one-tenth of the Earth's surface.
18. Zambia gets its name from this waterbody.
19. The famous Calico Museum is located in this city.
20. This actor's original name was Shivaji Rao Gaekwad.
21. Peachick
22. Sleet
23. The leaves of this plant is used in the body-decorating process known as mehendi.
24. Neelam Sanjeeva Reddy was the first chief minister of the state.
25. Raksha, a she-wolf, suckled him.
26. These spouting hot springs are found mainly in the US and the Russian Far East.
27. This word is a blend of the words smoke and fog.
28. This ruler gave up warfare despite being victorious in the Kalinga War.
29. The world's largest body of natural fresh water
30. Samta Sthal
31. He wrote the book *Curries and Other Indian Dishes.*
32. Right Faith, Right Knowledge, Right Conduct
33. La Manche
34. In 1973, after eighteen years in exile, he was re-elected president of Argentina.
35. Baba Buddha was the first keeper of this religious book.

36. Sir Ronald Ross discovered it within the Anopheles mosquito in 1897.
37. It is divided into the Palaeolithic, Mesolithic and Neolithic Ages.
38. Their celebration is called a jamboree.
39. This marine measure is six feet in depth.
40. He was exiled on the island of Elba in 1814–15.
41. Snowline
42. Moa is an extinct bird that was native to this country.
43. The first UN Secretary-General from Africa.
44. The first empire to unite a great part of India under a central authority
45. Spun sugar on a stick
46. The flag of this country features the map of the country above two olive branches.
47. Trapezium
48. Yeti
49. Baht
50. In Hindi, I am known as 'adrak'.

Answers on pages 156–158

IQ

1. Which number should logically replace the question mark?

7	49	343	?	16807
1	2	3	4	5

2. If CRANE=RAN, then SPODE =?

3. Insert the missing number:
   196 (25) 324
   329 ( ) 137

4. Insert the missing number:
     ?   8
   39   13
     24   18

5. What should logically replace the question marks?

1	C	5	?
A	3	E	?

6. Find the odd one out.
   NIROY
   LEEST
   PORPEC
   NOBREZ

7. An anagram of this author's name is, very aptly, 'I'll make a wise phrase'. Who is he?

8. An express train leaves Kolkata for Mumbai at the same time as a passenger train leaves Mumbai for Kolkata. Which is farther from Kolkata when they meet? (Express train average speed: 60 km/hr; Passenger train average speed: 30 km/hr)

9. 100 cats killed 100 rats in three minutes. How many minutes did three cats take to kill three rats?

10. Which is the odd one out and why?
    ROFD
    RAGNUDAV
    TEYLENB
    METOC
    TAIF

11. Insert the word that completes the first word and starts the next. (Clue: Animal)
    C (...) X

12. If DRIVER = 7
    PEDESTRIAN = 11
    Then, ACCIDENT = ?

13. Find the number that logically completes the series: 2, 3, 5, 9, 17,_____

14. Use the digit '4' four times and the bracket, addition, subtraction, multiplication or division symbols to make the digit 3.

15. A zookeeper was asked to count the number of birds and animals in a zoo. He counted thirty heads and a hundred feet. Find the number of birds and the number of animals in the zoo.

16. Simplify this: The day before day after the day after the day before yesterday.

17. Does the last statement follow the first two?
    1. Marion is an Italian.
    2. Marion sings beautifully.
    3. All Italians sing beautifully.

18. Mr and Mrs Smith had seven sons. Each had a sister. How many people were there in the Smith family?

19. How much mud is there in a hole 1 foot by 2.5 feet by 3.75 feet?

20. Gloria has twelve right-hand gloves and fifteen left-hand gloves in a drawer. How many gloves should she take out to be sure of taking out at least one of each hand?

21. Find the next number in the sequence: 8, 15, 29, 57,
    ____

22. Rearrange the letters and find the odd one:
    EMEPLT
    QUOMSE
    EHOSU
    HURHCC

23. Ravi's watch is ten minutes slow, though he thinks it is five minutes fast. Rohan's watch is five minutes fast though he thinks it is ten minutes slow. They both plan to catch a train at 4 p.m. Who gets their first: Ravi or Rohan?

24. Assuming the truth of these sentences
    a) Yellow dogs are live animals.
    b) All live animals need food.
    Which of the following sentences is true?
    1) A dog is yellow because it needs food.
    2) All yellow dogs need food.
    3) Certain yellow dogs do not need food.
    4) Some yellow dogs are not live animals.

25. Why should a detective disbelieve this story? The spy entered the room, switched on the light, took a book from the shelf, and placed the secret note between pages 19 and 20.

26. Would it be cheaper to take one friend to the movies twice, or two friends at the same time?

27. Which number comes next in the series: 3, 8, 15, 24, 35_____

28. A test has twenty questions. If Peter gets 80 per cent correct, how many did he miss?

29. A zoo had 44 female and 36 male zebras. Which is the correct ratio of females to males?

30. Which number comes next in the series: 1, 1, 2, 3, 4, 9, 8_____

Answers on pages 158–159

SPEED ROUND

SET 1

1. Which fruit is 'Dusseri' a variety of: mango or jackfruit?
2. Which part of the word 'bifocals' means two?
3. Kajol is actress Dimple Kapadia's daughter: serious or joking?
4. Which card is used to predict one's future: Tarot card or Flash card?
5. How many zeroes are there in 10 crore (100 million)?
6. Which Indian prime minister was the son of another Indian prime minister?
7. What do even bald men wear to keep out the sun: caps or cravats?

SET 2

1. Calcium oxide is another name for: quicklime or quicksilver?
2. What was Shrek in the film series *Shrek*: a whale or an ogre?
3. Marble cakes are actually made of marble: serious or joking?

4. Besides Kapil Dev and Arjuna Ranatunga, who among these Asians captained his country to a World Cup victory: Wasim Akram or Imran Khan?
5. How many days are there in 144 hours?
6. To attain perfect bliss is to attain: nirvana or yoga?
7. In which country would you be in if you spent takas: Bhutan or Bangladesh?

SET 3
1. Normally, a violin has four, six or eight strings?
2. At Kanyakumari, there is a memorial to Swami Vivekananda or Netaji?
3. Against which country does Australia play the Border–Gavaskar Test series?
4. Which is a closer relative of the giraffe: the okapi or the zebra?
5. What was the name of Babur's father: Umar Sheikh Mirza or Omar Abdullah?
6. Which mythical ruler had the 'golden touch'?
7. Which word is used to describe signatures given by celebrities to their fans?

SET 4
1. Complete this trio of Indian music composers: Shankar, _____ and Loy.
2. Salt is used to preserve food: serious or joking?
3. The Solang Valley is in Himachal Pradesh or Arunachal Pradesh?
4. A cycling competition is usually held in: an aerodrome or a velodrome?
5. What does an oviparous mammal lay?

6. Red is a primary colour or a secondary colour?
7. Kalidas wrote in Sanskrit or in Urdu?

SET 5

1. The presence of which element makes the blood red: iron or copper?
2. What is the main ingredient of chopsuey: noodles or rice?
3. The Sundarbans is situated in a valley or a delta?
4. Which is a type of dyeing technique: Ikkat or Pashmina?
5. If you aren't careful, in which of these games can you go bankrupt: Ludo or Monopoly?
6. North African, Somali, Masai and South African are subspecies of which large bird?
7. S.D. Burman composed the music for *Sholay*: serious or joking?

SET 6

1. Which is the principal river of Myanmar: Irrawaddy or Meghna?
2. Which egg dish has two Ts, three Es, and one L in its name?
3. In Hindu mythology, who is considered to be the king of heaven?
4. Who has scored the fastest 6,000 runs in Test cricket?
5. Who is the first Indian prime minister to hold office for more than one term?
6. Which four-letter word is used to describe the male protagonist of a film?
7. In which city are the headquarters of the United Nations located?

SET 7

1. According to legend, Newton discovered gravity after what fell on his head?
2. Which country is known for its dykes: Holland or Spain?
3. Which character was created by Charles Dickens: Oliver Twist or Tom Brown?
4. The local name of the Indian wild dog sounds like which percussion instrument?
5. Which London-based football club has been coached by Arsene Wenger?
6. Which ray does the Chandra Telescope use to photograph galaxies?
7. Pakistan has a larger population than Russia: serious or joking?

SET 8

1. In tennis, which is the first Grand Slam tournament played in a calendar year: US Open or Australian Open?
2. Which famous Steven Spielberg film began with a woman being killed by a great white shark?
3. Which religious place is famous for its ghats: Sarnath or Varanasi?
4. Who has served as the chief minister of Madhya Pradesh: Rabri Devi or Uma Bharti?
5. What is a four-letter word for a killer whale?
6. What is the STD code for New Delhi?
7. Which comet is named after a contemporary of Sir Isaac Newton?

SET 9

1. Against which team did Steve Waugh make his Test debut: England or India?
2. Who was the first Indian woman to become the president of the Indian National Congress?
3. What would you call the official residence of an ambassador?
4. Who was the leading lady in M.F. Hussain's *Meenaxi: A Tale of Three Cities*?
5. Sikkim lies between Nepal and Bhutan: serious or joking?
6. In India, which is the highest peacetime gallantry award: Param Vir Chakra or Ashok Chakra?
7. What happens to its temperature when an animal wakes up from hibernation?

SET 10

1. Who is a Pakistani fast bowler: Danish Kaneria or Mohammad Sami?
2. Are horses herbivorous or carnivorous?
3. The famous Gahirmatha beach in Orissa is located on which Indian coast: east or west?
4. Which Paul wrote the bestselling book *The Population Bomb*: Ehrlich or Wood?
5. What kind of tube sticks out from the front of a kettle: snout, spout or tout?
6. Who is also known as the Tiger of Mysore?
7. Who is an expert at conducting an orchestra: Zakir Hussain or Zubin Mehta?

SET 11

1. Is Parthiv Patel a left-handed or a right-handed batsman?
2. Which Leo wrote the books *Anna Karenina* and *War and Peace*?
3. All leopards have spots: serious or joking?
4. In Hindu mythology, who was Pandu's wife: Kunti or Gandhari?
5. Which tiny particle has about the same mass as a proton: neutron or electron?
6. Which Indian state is bordered by Andhra Pradesh, Karnataka and Kerala?
7. Which actress made her debut in the film *Pardes*: Shilpa Shetty or Mahima Choudhary?

SET 12

1. Are ants classified as social, anti-social or socialist insects?
2. The Vidarbha Cricket Association Stadium is located in which city in Maharashtra: Ahmedabad or Nagpur?
3. Which water body is associated with the word 'Persian': bay or gulf?
4. Which of these places did an American reach first: the moon or space?
5. In a calendar year, which of these countries makes more films: India or the UK?
6. Which of these prizes has lesser number of categories: Nobel or Pulitzer?
7. What was Aristotle's nationality: Greek or Roman?

SET 13

1. Cabbages are always green in colour: serious or joking?
2. Who among these was the captain of the Indian Under-19 team: Sourav Ganguly or Mohammad Kaif?
3. Which of these is a reptile: an iguana or an echidna?
4. Which mountain range is broadly divided into the Canadian, Northern, Middle and Southern?
5. What does the 'O' in OPEC stand for?
6. Where did Vasco da Gama establish the first Portuguese factory: Cochin or Visakhapatnam?
7. Which scientist coined the name 'oxygen'?

SET 14

1. Name the first subatomic particle to be discovered by J.J. Thomson?
2. In the Mahabharata, what was the name of Nakula and Sahadeva's mother?
3. Blue and Green are different species of which bird: peacock or parrot?
4. Which of these rivers flows into the Bay of Bengal: Sharavathi or Godavari?
5. Which of these countries is a member of SAARC: Pakistan or Germany?
6. With which letter do the names of most films directed by Rakesh Roshan start: 'K' or 'R'?
7. The official residence of the prime minister of India is in New Delhi or Mumbai?

SET 15

1. Which of these has Sachin Tendulkar played more of: Tests or One Day Internationals?
2. Which of these is chiefly used to make platinum alloys: iridium or radium?
3. Which famous astrologer was born in 1503 and died in 1566?
4. Both the names of which Indian state and its capital start with the letter G?
5. Some owls are also active during the day: serious or joking?
6. Complete the title of this Hindi film: *Jo Jeeta Wohi*_____
7. Who was Gandhari's brother: Kamsa or Shakuni?

SET 16

1. In the works by Agatha Christie, what was Miss Marple's first name?
2. Mg is the symbol of which chemical element: manganese or magnesium?
3. Which of these rivers flows through the states of Karnataka and Tamil Nadu: Cauvery or Narmada?
4. In India, what is supposed to happen on a national scale every ten years: census or elections?
5. In the abbreviation NATO, what does 'N' stand for?
6. Which insect is also known as 'white ant'?
7. In cricket, what kind of illegal delivery would you bowl when you overstep?

SET 17

1. Which term relates to horses: equine or porcine?

2. The Nag river flows by Nagpur: serious or joking?
3. Shah Shuja and Aurangzeb were the sons of which Mughal emperor: Shah Jahan or Jahangir?
4. In comics, Popeye and Brutus compete with each other for whose affection?
5. The Ranji Trophy was named after which former cricketer?
6. What would a Chinese individual do with a won ton?
7. How is Rahul Gandhi related to Feroze Varun Gandhi?

SET 18

1. What does 'I' in FBI stand for: Intelligence or Investigation?
2. A chipmunk is a squirrel or a rabbit?
3. Which of these hill stations is located in Tamil Nadu: Ooty or Nainital?
4. Which four-letter word is another name for 'making bread shorter': trim or trip?
5. In 2001, which Australian became the youngest man to be ranked world number one in tennis?
6. Who said, 'Science is a wonderful thing if one does not have to earn one's living at it'?
7. What are Basmati and Manipuri different varieties of: roti or rice?

SET 19

1. Which of these rivers rises in the Maikala range in Madhya Pradesh: Krishna or Narmada?
2. What is Lord Krishna's panchajanya: a conch shell or a mace?

3. Which language is spoken by more people in Egypt: Urdu or Arabic?
4. Which ruler died while leading his troops on the battlefield: Tipu Sultan or Humayun?
5. What would you call an ice cream that has fruits in it: candy or tutti-frutti?
6. Which is used to measure depth: a fathom or a farad?
7. For contribution in which field is the Arjuna Award given?

SET 20

1. Which state is larger in area: Chhattisgarh or Madhya Pradesh?
2. Which Indian actor has an Italian father: John Abraham or Dino Morea?
3. Which country's ancient emperors held the title Mikado?
4. In cricket, which continent has the most number of Test-playing nations?
5. What is the present name of the city where Aung San Suu Kyi was born?
6. What is nearly equal to 2.54 cm: an inch or a foot?
7. What term is used to describe words or drawing scribbled on a wall: graffiti or cartoon?

SET 21

1. In India, how is a flag flown when there is a state mourning: full mast or half mast?
2. Which unit of weight is one-sixteenth of a pound: a gram or an ounce?
3. The name of which mountain pass means 'piles of dead bodies': Rohtang or Nathu La?

4. Which country did gymnast Nadia Comaneci represent at the Olympics: USA or Romania?
5. Which Shakespearean play is also known as 'the Scottish play'?
6. Which is a flattened Indian bread: kalakand or naan?
7. Who was the great grandfather of Aurangzeb: Babur or Akbar?

SET 22

1. Which hill station is in Uttarakhand: Mussoorie or Manali?
2. In India, how are 'cabs' mostly known?
3. Callisto and Europa are moons of Jupiter: serious or joking?
4. Michael Vaughan captained which team in Test cricket?
5. Which is usually found underwater: a sloth or an oyster?
6. Which folk art is from Bihar: Bidri or Madhubani?
7. Who was the only Indian Governor-General of independent India?

SET 23

1. What number shirt did Pelé wear during his football career?
2. Who starred in the film *Khakee*: Amitabh Bachchan or Aamir Khan?
3. Which is the twin city of Hyderabad: Aurangabad or Secunderabad?
4. Which dance form originated in Kerala: Theyyam or Chhau?

5. Apart from 'Entry' which other signage starting with 'E' are you most likely to see inside a cinema?
6. Which part of the body does pneumonia mainly affect?
7. From where did Shivaji escape by hiding inside a basket: Lucknow or Agra?

SET 24

1. Who, along with Rahul Dravid, was awarded the Padma Shri in 2004: Virender Sehwag or Sourav Ganguly?
2. Which colour comes between yellow and red in a rainbow?
3. The Niagara Falls partly lies in: Canada or Alaska?
4. The deficiency of which element is the cause of the most common type of goitre?
5. Who is known as the father of geometry: Euclid or Aristotle?
6. Which famous Italian food item literally means 'pie' ?
7. Raj Ghat is the samadhi of which leader?

SET 25

1. Which Indian philosopher started an ashram in Pondicherry: Sri Aurobindo or Ramanuja?
2. The Bara Imambara is in which Indian city: Panjim or Lucknow?
3. The alloy nickel silver is composed of zinc, nickel and which other metal?
4. Which is an Indian dessert: jalebi or zaffran?
5. Which colour is associated with the Dutch royal family: magenta or orange?

6. What did Omar Khayyam write: *Rubbaiyat* or *Shahmat*?
7. Which game in India is normally associated with 'tip cat': gilli danda or Ludo?

SET 26
1. Which is closer to Delhi: Bhopal or Hyderabad?
2. How many women have been president of the US?
3. In Hindu mythology, what is the name of Shiva's bull?
4. How many sides does a nonagon have?
5. What is the principal ingredient of omelettes?
6. What is the principal food of a giant panda?
7. What is the colour of Snow White's hair?

SET 27
1. Which is closer to Mumbai: Pune or Panaji?
2. Is zari work usually gold work or bronze work?
3. A wind vane shows the direction to or from where the wind is blowing?
4. In which continent is Spain located?
5. Which geometric instrument is used to draw arcs and circles?
6. Rajaraja I belonged to which dynasty: Cholas, Chalukyas or Hoysalas?
7. After which leader is the international airport of New Delhi named?

SET 28
1. Is Patna on the Ganga or the Brahmaputra?
2. Which is not a vertebrate: a python or a snail?
3. Maharashtra is the most populous state in India: serious or joking?

4. Which superhero's relative said: 'With great power comes great responsibility'?
5. If the Aussies are Australians, who are the Springboks?
6. Which is the study of the human skeleton: anatomy or astronomy?
7. Whose pet dog is Pluto?

SET 29

1. Is the Krishna river mainly in Andhra Pradesh or Tamil Nadu?
2. What does the red circle on the Japanese flag represent?
3. Cinderella's coach was made from a guava: serious or joking?
4. How many full sleeves do thirty yellow shirts have?
5. By which name was the empress Mihr-un-nisa better known?
6. Which director is common to the films *Mr India* and *Bandit Queen*?
7. What kind of birds provided early airmail services?

SET 30

1. A cube has: four, six or eight faces?
2. A hinge joint joins your arm and shoulder: serious or joking?
3. Is Cherrapunji in Assam or Meghalaya?
4. Normally, which colour comes just before green in traffic lights?
5. Which is the first month in the Saka calendar?
6. Which year was the last leap year before 2002 CE?

7. Expand the acronym UFO.

SET 31
1. Was the film *Roja* first made in Hindi or Tamil?
2. Who was the first Indian prime minister of the twentieth century?
3. Which Italian city has a famous leaning tower?
4. What colour does blue litmus paper turn when put in acid?
5. Are your vocal chords in your larynx or your trachea?
6. The Arctic Circle is near the North Pole or the South Pole?
7. In computers, what are Garamond, Century and Verdana different types of?

SET 32
1. Do we usually have one kidney or a pair of kidneys?
2. Sushmita Sen is Amartya Sen's daughter: serious or joking?
3. In Hindu mythology, who was also known as Panchali?
4. How many sides does a parallelogram have?
5. What does a chauffeur do for a living?
6. What fungus do bakers use?
7. What colour cap is awarded to English Test cricketers?

SET 33
1. What do antiques refer to?
2. A perimeter and boundary can mean the same thing: serious or joking?
3. What is pressed while changing gears: clutch or brake?

4. Which part of a mint plant is used to make mint sauce?
5. How many of your forty-six chromosomes usually come from your mother?
6. Who became the youngest heavyweight boxing champion in 1986 but spent 1994 in jail?
7. What is the capital of the state of South Australia: Adelaide or Melbourne?

SET 34

1. Gujarat lies east of Madhya Pradesh: serious or joking?
2. Would water on Pluto boil or freeze?
3. Generally, how many wheels does a cycle rickshaw have?
4. Who erected twelve altars to the twelve Olympian gods on the Hyphasis, the present-day Beas?
5. How many minutes to 2 p.m. is it when it is 12.50 p.m.?
6. Which colour shirt did the cricketers wear while playing in the first Cricket World Cup?
7. What does 'R' stand for on a car's gear stick?

SET 35

1. Lungfish really have lungs: serious or joking?
2. Which narrow bones form the cage around your heart and lungs?
3. Who was the first British prime minister to have a husband?
4. Does a rhombus have three, four or five sides?
5. Which is an Arab ship with a large triangular sail: dhow or kayak?

6. How many rings are there in the top row of the Olympic flag?
7. Which telephone sound can also be worn on the finger?

SET 36

1. Most idlis are made from rice or wheat?
2. On what animal did Rani Lakshmibai do most of her fighting?
3. Nocturnal animals are active during the day or night?
4. Which is the second largest ocean in terms of size?
5. Which animal was earlier called 'camelopard': giraffe or leopard?
6. How many wisdom teeth do adult humans usually have: three, four, five or six?
7. What is the opposite of explosion?

SET 37

1. What do we call a space that contains no air or any other particles?
2. Is upma usually sweet or salty?
3. Which is longer: the small or the large intestine?
4. Shanti Van is the samadhi of which prime minister of India?
5. Little Miss Muffet feared spiders: serious or joking?
6. Which insects are kept in an apiary?
7. A pentathlon has five, ten or fifteen events?

SET 38

1. In which Shakespearean play would you meet characters named Ariel, Prospero, Miranda and

Caliban: *The Merchant of Venice, The Tempest* or *Richard III*?
2. What name is given to the line that forms a circle?
3. Is Ooty in the Nilgiris or Aravallis?
4. The dance form Kuchipudi originated in West Bengal: serious or joking?
5. Which is the human body's largest gland?
6. What colour does copper turn to if left outdoors?
7. What is the study or collection of coins, paper currency and medals called?

SET 39
1. A crore is ten million: serious or joking?
2. Which colour forms the background of the flag of the UN?
3. Who was the first American to go to space: Neil Armstrong or Alan Shepard?
4. Which country separates Alaska from most of the other states of the US?
5. Which great Indian leader's surname sounds like a religious mark on the forehead?
6. Which cartoon duck celebrated his sixtieth birthday in 1994?
7. Spider hermit and horseshoe are varieties of which creature?

SET 40
1. The India Gate is in Mumbai: serious or joking?
2. Which sport is played in India's Durand Cup?
3. What is informally called a chopper: a tram or a helicopter?

4. How many legs does an adult fly have?
5. What carries blood away from the heart?
6. What is measured on a spring balance?
7. From which famous town did the Pied Piper take away all the children?

SET 41

1. In the nursery rhyme 'Hey Diddle Diddle', who ran away with the spoon?
2. A meteorologist studies meteors: serious or joking?
3. Which country did Moses lead his people out of?
4. Which is not a martial art: kung fu, ikebana or judo?
5. Which continent has half the world's population?
6. When you inhale, does your chest expand or contract?
7. Who composed the music for the film *Roja*?

SET 42

1. What was the most common colour of tennis balls before yellow was introduced?
2. Louis Braille was born blind: serious or joking?
3. If Juhu beach is in Maharashtra, where is Chowpatty?
4. What do you call the result of multiplying two numbers?
5. Who wrote the science fiction classic *Rendezvous with Rama*?
6. When you add a post-script to a letter, which two letters of the alphabet do you use?
7. Who was Karishma Kapoor's grandfather?

SET 43

1. Which colour is used to describe cinema tickets bought illegally?

2. In which country was Sir Donald Bradman born?
3. Which famous Dickens character's stepfather was Mr Edward Murdstone?
4. Flying foxes are bats: serious or joking?
5. Between 543 CE and 755 CE, which dynasty had their capital at Badami?
6. What is the highest number on a telephone keypad?
7. If tea is made from leaves, what is coffee made from?

SET 44

1. What is the study of flags called?
2. Wales is a part of Great Britain: serious or joking?
3. How many years are there in three decades?
4. In the acronym ESP, what does 'E' stand for?
5. Who created Sherlock Holmes: P.D. James or Arthur Conan Doyle?
6. The mridangam is a wind, percussion or stringed instrument?
7. What does 'merci' mean when translated from French to English?

SET 45

1. How many seconds are there in a day?
2. Who was evil: Dr Jekyll or Mr Hyde?
3. A drake is a male horse: serious or joking?
4. The people of which Asian country refer to their country as Druk-Yul meaning 'Land of the Dragon'?
5. Is the scapula above or below the femur?
6. How long will it take a car to travel 150 km at an average speed of 30 kmph?

7. Who was the captain of the 1983 team which won the Cricket World Cup for India?

SET 46

1. Which organization employs more people: Indian Airlines or Indian Railways?
2. Bats hang upside down when asleep: serious or joking?
3. How many kilometres are there in a centimetre if the scale on a map is 75 km to the cm?
4. Which brothers achieved the first powered, sustained, and controlled airplane flight?
5. What would ache if you had a migraine?
6. Which actor was affectionately called 'Kaka': Rajesh Khanna or Shammi Kapoor?
7. Who was the 'chief' of the losing team at the Battle of Plassey?

SET 47

1. Does Brahma sit on a lotus or a rose?
2. Only female Anopheles mosquitoes can transmit malaria: serious or joking?
3. What is the highest point on a mountain called?
4. Which is called a 'feline': a cat, a dog or a horse?
5. How many sides does a hexagon have?
6. Which country is the second largest producer of silk?
7. Comics: What is Blondie and Dagwood's surname?

SET 48

1. Which satellite orbited the Earth first: Sputnik or Explorer I?

2. Termites belong to a group of cellulose-eating insects: serious or joking?
3. Along the banks of which river is Agra located?
4. The word 'nasal' would describe which part of your body?
5. In cricket, how many runs are scored if a six is hit from a no ball?
6. Which of Batman's friends sounds like a bird?
7. Besides Indira Gandhi, name another woman prime minister of India.

SET 49
1. A stallion is a male horse: serious or joking?
2. Which is taller: the Qutb Minar or the Shahid Minar?
3. Who became the king of Kishkindha immediately after Bali's death?
4. Which key on a computer keyboard sounds like you have changed position?
5. Who is the first actor to receive three consecutive Filmfare Awards in the Best Actor category?
6. On which part of your body might you wear pumps?
7. In which sport is there a scrum: rugby or hockey?

SET 50
1. Who was president of the US immediately before Bill Clinton?
2. In a beehive, only female bees work: serious or joking?
3. Which country hosted the 2000 Olympic Games?
4. How many sides does a heptagon have?
5. Which of these has no known function in humans: appendix or liver?

6. The Hawaii Islands are a part of which country?
7. In *Raja Hindustani*, who played the role of the Aarti Sehgal?

Answers on pages 160–174

FUN FACTS 5

1. The rhinoceros beetle can lift an object 850 times its own weight.
2. The first Indian film released in English was *Karma* (1933). Devika Rani, Rabindranath Tagore's grand-niece, made her debut in the film as the leading lady.
3. The youngest Nobel laureate in Literature, Rudyard Kipling, was born in Bombay.
4. The naval habit of naming ships after women inspired Clement Wragge to name hurricanes after women in the nineteenth century.
5. Masadur Rahman Baidya of Kolkata, who lost both his legs in an accident, swam the English Channel in 1997.
6. Fort William College was founded by the East India Company to teach British civil servants the laws, customs, religions, languages and literatures of India for administrative benefits.
7. Sautè, a method of cooking on high heat, comes from the French word for 'jumped'.
8. German pacifist and journalist Carl von Ossietzky, Burmese politician Aung San Suu Kyi and Chinese human rights activist Liu Xiaobo are three Nobel

laureates who have been under arrest at the time of receiving the award.

9. In the human body, the stomach gets a new lining every three to four days. The strong acids the stomach uses to digest food would otherwise also digest the stomach.

10. The Silver Revolution is associated with an increase in the production of eggs or poultry in India.

11. The two main tributaries of the Nile River are the White Nile and the Blue Nile. Both of them get their names from the colour of their water.

12. Earth's only natural satellite is simply called the moon because people didn't know other moons existed until Galileo Galilei discovered four moons orbiting Jupiter in 1610.

ANSWERS

INDIA

1. Arunachal Pradesh
2. Jantar Mantar
3. C.V. Raman
4. Flute
5. Chanakya or Kautilya
6. Mahatma Gandhi's ashes
7. Sushmita Sen
8. Akbar
9. Rajiv Gandhi
10. Kerala
11. India Gate
12. The Sun Temple, Konark
13. Satyameva Jayate
14. 'Saare jahan se achcha'
15. Bihu
16. Rajasthan
17. Mumbai
18. Mahatma Gandhi
19. Kolkata Metro
20. Parsi

21. Kathak
22. Morarji Desai
23. Amritsar
24. Karnataka
25. The President's Bodyguard
26. J.R.D. Tata
27. Shah Jahan
28. M.S. Subbulakshmi
29. Uttar Pradesh
30. Pipal or bodhi tree
31. Uttar Pradesh
32. Mother Teresa
33. Baba Amte
34. Coconut palm
35. Razia Sultana
36. Maharana Kumbha
37. Ten
38. Pandit Ravi Shankar
39. Haldi
40. Andhra Pradesh
41. Damodar Valley Corporation, also known as DVC
42. Rakesh Sharma
43. R.K. Laxman
44. Trams
45. Kerala
46. Green
47. Haryana
48. Mughal
49. Swaraj
50. Rajasthan

GEOGRAPHY

1. Patna
2. Karakoram
3. Turkey
4. Formosa
5. Stalingrad
6. Bangkok
7. The Philippines
8. Mozambique
9. Africa
10. East Berlin and West Berlin
11. New York City
12. Germany
13. Falkland Islands
14. Paris
15. Siachen Glacier
16. Sutlej
17. Switzerland
18. Belgium
19. All are beaches in Goa.
20. Liberia. The capital is Monrovia.
21. Greenland
22. Kalahari
23. Jordan
24. Russia
25. Six
26. Gerardus Mercator
27. Delta
28. Manhattan Island
29. Andes
30. Tigris

31. Clouds
32. Denmark
33. Pakistan
34. The carved heads of former US presidents George Washington, Thomas Jefferson, Abraham Lincoln and Theodore Roosevelt at Mount Rushmore.
35. Tanganyika and Zanzibar
36. Caspian Sea
37. Lion
38. Zambezi
39. Italy
40. New York City
41. Jordan
42. France
43. Venice
44. Orange
45. Wellington
46. Antarctica
47. Riyadh
48. Ho Chi Minh City
49. Mediterranean Sea
50. Amazon

ENTERTAINMENT
1. M.S. Subbulakshmi
2. Shabana Azmi
3. Tansen
4. Bruce Wayne/Batman
5. Michael Jackson
6. Pandit Ravi Shankar
7. Ben Kingsley

8. Ronald and Nancy Reagan
9. Jurassic Park
10. A documentary on rockstars and rock music
11. Amjad Khan
12. Devika Rani
13. Dhanno
14. Harrison Ford
15. *Pather Panchali*
16. Meerkat
17. Ritwik Ghatak
18. Watziznehm or Kisasa
19. Donald Duck
20. Spiders
21. Amitabh Bachchan
22. A dolphin
23. Tom Cruise
24. Syed Kirmani (It also featured cricketer Sandip Patil.)
25. Cats in the *Top Cat* series
26. Captain Spock
27. Macaulay Culkin
28. *The Ten Commandments*
29. Laurel and Hardy
30. Sanjeev Kumar
31. Zakir Hussain
32. Satyajit Ray
33. Mehmood
34. *Maine Pyar Kiya*
35. Ventriloquist
36. *Aladdin*
37. An anchor
38. James Bond

39. Zakir Hussain
40. *The Sound of Music*
41. Mithun Chakraborty
42. Amitabh Bachchan (He had a triple role.)
43. Charlie Chaplin
44. Sridevi
45. Kumar Sanu
46. *Gandhi*
47. Charlton Heston
48. Satyajit Ray
49. Policeman
50. Naseeruddin Shah

WHAT'S THE QUESTION 1

1. Where does Miss Marple live?
2. What word is used to describe a person who has a mania for stealing things?
3. What is the singular form of the word 'data'?
4. What is the white portion of an egg called?
5. What is the name of the gorilla in *The Black Island*?
6. What do we call a squirrel's nest?
7. What do you call the lines on a map that connect places receiving the same amount of rainfall in a given period?
8. What is the name of the ancient trade route between China and the West?
9. In the World Wrestling Federation, what is Shawn Michaels' nickname?
10. What do you call words written on a tombstone?
11. Who is Robin Hood?
12. Name three types of honeybees.
13. What was actor Ashok Kumar's nickname?

14. What instrument is used to measure the speed of wind?
15. Who is Björn Borg?
16. What is a muzzle?
17. What is a boomerang?
18. Why was the Eiffel Tower erected?
19. What is the day after Christmas popularly known as?
20. In which park do Yogi Bear and Boo Boo live?
21. What is a receipt?
22. In a right-angled triangle, what do you call the side opposite the right angle?
23. What is music composer A.R. Rahman's real name?
24. In the Ramayana, who was Sumitra?
25. What is the popular name for a mixture of concentrated nitric and hydrochloric acids, used for dissolving gold?
26. Name the three parts of the small intestine.
27. What is isabgol?
28. What is a modem?
29. What are a bird of prey's hooked claws called?
30. What is used to raise a car when a tyre needs changing?
31. Who is Kanga?
32. Who is Karan Johar?
33. What is the name of a well-known West African trade wind?
34. What is the medical term for chicken pox?
35. Who is V.S. Naipaul?
36. What is Taurus?
37. What do you call the storey of a building which is between the two main floors?
38. Name the British archaeologist who discovered the largely intact tomb of King Tutankhamen.
39. By what name was Namibia formerly known?

40. By what other name is rabies known?
41. What is a tannery?
42. What is Hampi?
43. What do you call a piece of art made by sticking different materials such as photographs and pieces of paper or fabric on to a surface?
44. Who was the lovable alien ET?
45. Who was James Prescott Joule?
46. Who were Cinderella's stepsisters?
47. What is the stomach?
48. Who is Mandrake?
49. What is the Greek name for Greece and appears on its stamps?
50. Who was Le Corbusier?

MIXED BAG 1

1. The rickshaw
2. Wall Street
3. P.V. Narasimha Rao
4. Mount Everest
5. A male horse and a female donkey
6. Akbar
7. Rabindranath Tagore
8. Scrabble
9. Muscles
10. *A Suitable Boy* by Vikram Seth
11. One Member One Vote
12. Silk
13. Piloting
14. Silencer
15. Writing a computer virus

16. To prevent the pockets from tearing under the weight of tools and to increase their durability
17. Hands
18. Crater
19. Santa Claus
20. The Pope
21. A police van
22. Manhattan Project
23. Rukmini Devi Arundale
24. January
25. Mouse
26. The head
27. The trumpet
28. Gujarat
29. Twenty-one
30. Health
31. Over-the-counter drugs. Medicines which are available without a prescription.
32. Agra Fort
33. Greenpeace
34. Mercury
35. Gold
36. They are all diamonds.
37. New York
38. Japan
39. One litre
40. The moon
41. An ambulance
42. Glass
43. P.V. Narasimha Rao
44. Read Only Memory

45. The Golden Temple
46. M.F. Hussain
47. Reforestation
48. Half a byte
49. Jeans
50. Alexander Graham Bell

WHO AM I?

1. Mickey Mouse
2. Gautama Buddha
3. Alfred Hitchcock
4. Albert Einstein
5. Richie Rich
6. Jawaharlal Nehru
7. Otto Von Bismarck
8. Abhimanyu
9. Adam
10. Sir Garfield Sobers
11. Prithviraj Chauhan
12. Enid Blyton
13. Subhas Chandra Bose
14. Archimedes
15. Tintin
16. Queen Elizabeth II
17. Tom Brown
18. Rudyard Kipling
19. Thomas Alva Edison
20. Alexander the Great
21. Mark Twain
22. Amitabh Bachchan
23. Dr S. Radhakrishnan

24. Obelix
25. Mira Nair

LANGUAGE AND LITERATURE

1. *A Christmas Carol*
2. R.K. Narayan
3. *Wuthering Heights*
4. Naipaul
5. Munshi Premchand
6. Scorpion
7. *Les Misérables*
8. Mark Twain
9. Agatha Christie
10. Tom Sawyer
11. Robin Hood
12. Scamper
13. *Moby Dick*
14. Sherlock Holmes
15. The name of the cow that Jack traded for some beans.
16. *Gulliver's Travels*
17. Maps
18. Leo Tolstoy
19. Limerick
20. Going to be sold at an auction
21. Governors-General
22. Nautilus
23. *Grimms' Fairy Tales*
24. Brown bear
25. *The Count of Monte Cristo*
26. *Gitanjali* by Rabindranath Tagore
27. A person who spends a great deal of time watching

television and almost no time exercising.
28. Lewis Carroll
29. 'If' by Rudyard Kipling
30. Malgudi
31. And
32. Charles Dickens
33. Twenty years
34. *Black Beauty*
35. The Queen of Hearts (*Alice's Adventures in Wonderland*)
36. *The Hunchback of Notre Dame*
37. *The Wonderful Wizard of Oz*
38. Karaoke
39. Obituary
40. Antonio
41. Chit
42. Hans Christian Andersen
43. *Treasure Island*
44. Peter Pan
45. *Animal Farm* by George Orwell
46. It is so named because of the red or pink tape used to bind and secure official documents.
47. Anne Frank
48. *Little Women*
49. An arrangement or understanding which is based upon the trust of both or all parties, rather than being legally binding.
50. Brunch

WHAT'S THE QUESTION 2

1. How would you express the number 1090 in Roman numerals?

2. What is the nose?
3. What is the term used to describe the process of caring for and beautifying the feet?
4. Who was Dushala?
5. Name Quasimodo's three gargoyle friends in the Walt Disney film *The Hunchback of Notre Dame*.
6. What was the name of the chalice (cup) used at Jesus's Last Supper?
7. Name the most northerly pass that connects Pakistan and Afghanistan.
8. Who was the first US astronaut to orbit the Earth?
9. How many knights belonged to King Arthur's round table?
10. What is the medical term for baldness?
11. What do you call a narrow strip of land with sea on either side, joining two larger masses of land?
12. What do you call the scientific study of birds?
13. What do you call a trench filled with water that surrounds a castle?
14. What is a large French country house or castle called?
15. What is the Indian (Hindi) name for tamarind?
16. Who is Peter Pan?
17. What was the original name of table tennis?
18. Who is Donald Duck?
19. Who were the creators of the first motion picture?
20. Who is Dalai Lama?
21. Who is James Bond?
22. What is Capricorn?
23. What is Panchatantra?
24. What is the height of the mountain K2 or Godwin Austen?

25. What is the name of the hot southerly wind on the northern slopes of the Alps?
26. What term is used to describe the application of gold or silver on a surface in a fine pattern?
27. What was the original name of volleyball?
28. In Roman mythology, how is Cupid (the god of love) depicted?
29. Which organizations are responsible for awarding the Nobel Prizes every year?
30. Where did Gandhiji give his 'Quit India' call during the freedom movement?
31. What is the currency of the United Arab Emirates and Morocco?
32. What is the French national anthem called?
33. In which ship did Francis Drake sail around the world?
34. What is the French equivalent of 'thank you very much'?
35. What is the Big Bang theory?
36. Name one of Spider-Man's enemies.
37. What is the human version of Mad Cow Disease called?
38. Name a famous book on films written by Satyajit Ray.
39. Name a famous painting by Pablo Picasso.
40. What is the sport of BMX or Bicycle Motocross?
41. What is the name of the popular column written by Khushwant Singh?
42. Who was Lokmanya Tilak?
43. What is the first name of Prime Minister Deve Gowda?
44. Name some famous landmarks in Malgudi, the fictional town created by R.K. Narayan.
45. What is the full name of the club that owns and governs the Wimbledon tennis tournament?
46. Who is Mason Gamble?

47. What are the names of the uncles of Casper the Friendly Ghost?
48. What is a crescent-shaped sand dune called?
49. In the book of the same name, who were the last of the Mohicans?
50. What are the first and last letters of the Greek alphabet?

HISTORY

1. Panipat
2. Allaudin Khilji
3. Kolkata
4. Agra Fort
5. Jawaharlal Nehru
6. Oskar Schindler
7. Dr S. Radhakrishnan
8. Indira Gandhi
9. Rani Lakshmibai/Rani of Jhansi
10. The Taj Mahal
11. Mahatma Gandhi
12. Goa
13. Quit India Movement
14. Harshavardhana
15. Kanishka
16. Aurangabad
17. He was conferred the title 'Raja'.
18. Bastille
19. Slavery
20. The German attack on the (former) USSR in 1941
21. Winston Churchill
22. Belgium
23. Aristotle

24. Confucius
25. Japan
26. London
27. The eruption of the volcano Vesuvius
28. The International Committee of the Red Cross
29. The Statue of Liberty
30. The Hiroshima bombing
31. A tank
32. Soviet Union
33. Amelia Earhart
34. Pearl Harbour
35. Ghiyasuddin Balban
36. Nelson Mandela
37. Christopher Columbus
38. Mandalas
39. General Dupleix
40. Gol Gumbaz
41. The Chauri Chaura incident
42. The Statue of Liberty
43. Muhammad bin Tughluq
44. Shivaji
45. Akbar Shah II
46. The fiddle
47. Florence Nightingale
48. Adolf Hitler
49. Gautama Buddha
50. Nepal

FOOD
1. All of them are varieties of mangoes.
2. Fish

3. All of them are varieties of cheese.
4. Dum pukht
5. Wimbledon Tennis Championships
6. Kulcha
7. Parsis
8. Pestle
9. Carrot
10. Fish
11. Penguins are found in the Antarctic. Inuits live in the Arctic.
12. Papaya
13. Apple
14. Oliver Twist
15. Hamburger (from Hamburg)
16. Pasta
17. Vanilla
18. Biscuit
19. The finger
20. Buffet
21. All are types of soup.
22. Bhutta (maize)
23. Water
24. Ginger
25. Clay
26. Ketchup
27. Tomato
28. Milk
29. Shrimp
30. Supari
31. Grapes
32. Deer

33. Alphonso
34. Sanjeev Kapoor
35. Hot cross buns
36. Stir-fried noodles
37. Yeast
38. Kulfi
39. Dosa
40. Peanuts
41. Sundae
42. Spinach
43. Sugar
44. Falafel
45. Tea
46. Iodine
47. Room service
48. Marco Polo
49. Nutmeg
50. Yoghurt

SPOT THE ANSWER 1

1. c. A tadpole. The tadpole is the aquatic larval stage of an amphibian.
2. d. The Indian National Congress. It was founded on 28 December 1885, and played a major role in India's freedom struggle.
3. a. Punjab
4. d. Leaning Tower of Pisa
5. a. He is trapped in a cave and dies of starvation.
6. a. An expert at solving crossword puzzles
7. b. Tennis. She won the Junior Lawn Tennis Championship in 1966, Asian Lawn Tennis Championship in 1972, and

the All-India Hard Court Tennis Championship in 1974.

8. c. Based on the initials (BP) of its founder
9. c. Rani Lakshmibai of Jhansi
10. d. Sherlock Holmes
11. a. They were barred from buying land. The Maharaja of Kashmir forbade the British to own land in order to prevent them from assuming power, and the British built houseboats instead.
12. d. Satyagraha
13. b. Michael Jackson (Maikeru is Japanese for Michael)
14. b. It was coloured pink for the Prince of Wales's (King Edward VII) visit in 1876.
15. d. He put it in his father's coffin.
16. c. Being a champion marble player as a child
17. b. Fish
18. a. A crescent-shaped (bread-like) roll made of yeast
19. b. The correct term for a person who polishes shoes for a living
20. a. Bhopal
21. a. The YMCA. The Young Men's Christian Association is a world-wide Christian voluntary movement for women and men, seeking to build a community based on love, peace and reconciliation.
22. a. After Sir George Everest, the then Surveyor General of India. Sir George Everest was the Surveyor General of India in 1830–1843. He is credited with completing the trigonometric survey of India. Mount Everest was renamed in his honour, from Peak XV, in 1865.
23. a. Animals are slaughtered.
24. a. The Indian National Flag

25. a.   He misrepresented his age.
26. a.   She stole the Japanese royal flag at the Tokyo Olympics.
27. b.   The young of a hare
28. b.   A graveyard, because of the marble tombstones
29. b.   Production of fish
30. b.   A pre-Independence cricket tournament
31. b.   Coffee
32. a.   By ringing a bell
33. c.   Small dark flecks produced by the burning of powdered coal or other materials
34. d.   Michael Jackson
35. d.   Mahatma Gandhi. They were finally immersed in the holy Sangam in Allahabad.
36. d.   Colour-coded arrangements of knotted threads. The colours of the cords, the way the cords are connected together, the relative placement of the cords, the spaces between the cords, the types of knots on the individual cords, and the relative placement of the knots are all part of theological-numerical recording.
37. a.   Ashoka
38. d.   Paper. In the ISO paper size system, all pages have a height-to-width ratio of the square root of two (1:1.4142).
39. d.   Spaghetti Westerns. Popular in the '60s and '70s, Sergio Leone was one of the famous directors of such films, and Clint Eastwood one of the major actors in this genre.
40. a.   It was the house where Aung San Suu Kyi was kept under house arrest. She won the Nobel Peace prize in 1991.

41. a. Have a prosperous and happy new year.
42. b. Dhyan Chand's birthday. He was one of the greatest hockey players of all times.
43. b. To be licked. It is a Latin word.
44. b. They generally hunt at night.
45. d. Cook in it. (Chinese cooking vessel)
46. c. Due to smallpox
47. a. World Wildlife Fund
48. a. *Arabian Nights*
49. c. Akihito
50. c. Bloodhound

WHAT'S THE QUESTION 3

1. What is the name of the airport in Amsterdam?
2. What was unusual about the Oscar presented to Walt Disney for *Snow White and the Seven Dwarfs*?
3. What are the names of the electronic devices at Wimbledon which are used to judge net cords and serves?
4. In cricket, what is the term used for doctoring the ball at the seam to give it unnatural movement?
5. Who is Ruskin Bond?
6. Who gave the Koh-i-noor diamond its name?
7. What is the title of Michael Jackson's autobiography?
8. What is the name of Singapore's airport?
9. What is the currency of Myanmar (formerly Burma)?
10. Who defeated who at the Battle of Hastings (1066 CE)?
11. Besides JFK, name another airport in New York.
12. Who fought the Crimean War?
13. Who is Jane Austen?
14. What is the currency of Malaysia?
15. What were the first two of Hercules' Twelve Labours?

16. Who were the Cyclopes? (singular: Cyclops)
17. Who was Rajesh Khanna?
18. What is magic potion?
19. What is sometimes called the thirteenth sign of the zodiac?
20. What was the currency of the Netherlands until the introduction of the Euro in 2002?
21. When did World War I end?
22. How are hurricanes named?
23. Name Dhyan Chand's autobiography.
24. Who created Dracula?
25. What is 24 October celebrated as?
26. Which flag has green, white and red vertical stripes, with an eagle grasping a snake on the white portion?
27. What was the name of Charles Lindbergh's aircraft in which he made the first solo transatlantic flight?
28. What is a crossword?
29. What is the London address of Britain's Chancellor of the Exchequer?
30. What is kidney?
31. What is *Chitty-Chitty-Bang-Bang*?
32. Who patented the first successfully manufactured electric razor?
33. What is plague?
34. Where did the Wright brothers' first successful flight take place?
35. What happened in Kurukshetra?
36. What is another name for Piranha?
37. In the comic strip *Hagar the Horrible*, what is the name of Hagar's family duck?
38. Who was Henri Dunant?

39. Who was Megasthenes?
40. Name three species of penguin.
41. Name different varieties of oranges.
42. What is enamel?
43. What is Barbie's full name?
44. Who is Govind Nihalani?
45. What is the meaning of the word 'astronaut'?
46. What is the name given to a portable loose-leaf notebook?
47. What is a shoe_horn?
48. When was the walkman invented?
49. In summer, which hot, dry north Indian wind scorches the crops and grass?
50. What is a 'bit'?

SCIENCE
1. In the human body. They are the bones of the forearm.
2. Zinc. It is a metal. The others are alloys. Bronze is an alloy of copper and tin. Brass is an alloy of copper and zinc. Pewter is a tin-based alloy.
3. The smell is deliberately added so that people can detect leaks.
4. Marie Curie
5. Aspirin
6. Logarithms
7. Ozone
8. Newton. The others are computer languages.
9. Neptune
10. The sun
11. All of them are types of bridges.
12. Green

13. Africa
14. Garbage In, Garbage Out
15. AB+
16. Fahrenheit to Celsius
17. Gold
18. They are different types of fractures.
19. Telephone
20. Simple
21. Your armpits
22. None
23. Carbon paper
24. An equal and opposite reaction
25. Photosynthesis
26. Earth
27. Pierre and Marie Curie
28. Handwriting
29. The eye. It is caused by an increase in pressure within the eyeball, causing gradual loss of sight.
30. Because it has a high melting point
31. It cools the engine.
32. Jaundice
33. Echo
34. 360
35. Kidney
36. Zero and one
37. An electromagnet
38. The liver
39. Ringworm. It is a skin disease. Rest are all parasites.
40. Tin
41. The vacuum cleaner
42. There is no air inside.

43. Diamond
44. Mouse
45. You would not be able to speak. The larynx is also called the 'voice box'.
46. Earth
47. Rhombus
48. The lungs
49. He was the boy who was given the first vaccination against smallpox by Edward Jenner.
50. Smallpox

WILDLIFE
1. Australia
2. Giant panda
3. Common octopus
4. The grizzly bear
5. Gir Forest in Gujarat
6. Elsa
7. Python
8. Snow leopard
9. Drones
10. Lion
11. The horse
12. Kanha National Park
13. Birds that lay their eggs in other birds' nests and have the foster parents take care of them, e.g. cuckoo.
14. Three
15. The ostrich cannot fly.
16. Beaver
17. Mosquito
18. One. Cod is a fish. Jellyfish and crayfish are not fish.

19. Albatross
20. Elephant
21. Bison
22. King cobra
23. Keratin
24. Eggs
25. Tiger
26. Lizard
27. Liger
28. Dinosaur
29. Lay eggs
30. Keibul Lamjao National Park
31. Gharial (because of its bulbous nose)
32. Tails
33. Deer
34. Walrus
35. Seal
36. All of them are types of fox.
37. Cat
38. Brush
39. Bandicoot
40. Jaguar
41. Nilgai
42. Form
43. Madhya Pradesh
44. Blue whale
45. Spider
46. Nightingale
47. Dodo
48. The giant panda. The others carry their babies in their pouches.

49. Bear
50. On its feet

MIXED BAG 2

1. A skull
2. They were all left-handed.
3. The Indian Institute of Technology is situated in each of these cities.
4. *Mein Kampf* (My Struggle)
5. Rabindranath Tagore
6. Sri Lanka Rupavahini Corporation
7. Bismillah Khan
8. Nelson Mandela
9. Red
10. In a crossword puzzle
11. Telephone
12. 'I promise to pay the bearer the sum of ...'
13. Cleopatra
14. Sitar
15. H.H. Munro
16. Mumbai
17. Bachendri Pal
18. Vinayak
19. Anna Sewell
20. Akbar
21. Netaji Subhas Chandra Bose
22. Pipal
23. Rice
24. Adolf Hitler
25. Bhosle
26. The Sun Temple

27. Liaquat Ali Khan
28. Ladakh
29. Information and Broadcasting
30. Homi Bhabha
31. Tulsidas
32. Ashok Kumar
33. John F. Kennedy
34. 52
35. Mahatma Gandhi
36. Turtle
37. Lakshadweep
38. July
39. Jawaharlal Nehru
40. Dal Lake
41. Venus
42. Epsilon
43. They are both three-wheelers.
44. Operation Vijay
45. Jawaharlal Nehru
46. Akbar
47. Rabindranath Tagore
48. *Oliver Twist*
49. Protima Bedi
50. Hyderabad

SPORTS
1. Alexander Dityatin
2. Ayrton Senna
3. Bodyline
4. The mafia
5. Hiroshima in 1994
6. O.M. Nambiar

7. Boris Becker
8. Ferenc Puskás
9. Dennis Lillee
10. Motorsports
11. Two
12. Vulture, El Buitre
13. Croquet
14. East Bengal and Mohun Bagan
15. Chetan Sharma
16. Dibyendu Barua
17. Barbados
18. Football
19. Muhammad Ali
20. Basketball, in NBA
21. Clive Lloyd
22. Billie Jean King
23. All were wrestlers.
24. Narendra Hirwani
25. Mansur Ali Khan Pataudi
26. Anatoly Karpov
27. The host nation
28. High jump; the technique was Fosbury Flop, a then-unorthodox head-first, back-to-the-bar method of high jumping
29. David Gower
30. The cartoon of a sorrowful duck that appeared onscreen when anybody got out on zero.
31. Garrincha
32. They were paying too much attention to football and neglecting archery.
33. At the boundary directly behind the wicketkeeper

34. Platform and Springboard
35. E.A.S. Prasanna
36. Hungary
37. Basketball
38. The Azteca Stadium, Mexico City
39. Gold
40. The bishop
41. Football
42. Polo
43. England
44. First FIFA World Cup match played indoors
45. Czechoslovakia
46. He was run out.
47. One half for each of the teams
48. Allan Border
49. International Master
50. Franz Beckenbauer

SPOT THE ANSWER 2
1. d. Mahatma Gandhi
2. a. Lunar eclipse
3. a. Wear it
4. c. Afghanistan
5. d. From the Italian word for 'pressed out'
6. c. The number of visitors to a website
7. a. Madhubala
8. c. China
9. b. To tell other bees where to find food
10. c. Yitzhak Rabin. He was the prime minister of Israel and led peace negotiations with Palestine and neighbouring Arab countries.

11. a. To strum a stringed instrument. It is a small bit of teardrop-shaped or triangular plastic.
12. c. Popeye
13. b. His gloves
14. d. Monopoly. He described the game as capitalist.
15. d. Sun stands still
16. c. Monkeys
17. d. Perspiration
18. c. Dennis Bergkamp. He played for the national football team of Netherlands, as well as for clubs like Ajax and Arsenal.
19. d. Night blindness
20. b. A tournament in which competitors play in turn against each other
21. b. A pond of frozen ice in a crater
22. a. Pyramids of Giza
23. a. Jim Corbett
24. b. On the birth of Indira Gandhi
25. a. Whether to break the broad or narrow end of an egg
26. b. Mount Everest
27. b. India's former first lady Usha Narayanan
28. d. Arunachal Pradesh
29. d. Vasco da Gama
30. b. The raja of Puri
31. c. There is no difference.
32. b. Education
33. d. Kitchen cabinet
34. c. *101 Dalmatians*
35. a. Confucius
36. d. Homeopathy
37. d. Eat it. It is a Thai soup.

38. c. Sandalwood
39. b. Animal skins
40. a. The human brain
41. a. Spectacles
42. c. *David Copperfield*
43. c. One million
44. b. High jump
45. d. Ghatotkacha
46. a. Malaysia
47. a. *A Christmas Carol.* In the book, the miser Ebenezer Scrooge is visited by the Ghosts of Christmas Past, Present, and Yet to Come.
48. b. South America
49. a. Brain
50. b. Koh-i-noor diamond

WHAT'S THE QUESTION 4

1. Who inspired Daniel Defoe to write *Robinson Crusoe*?
2. What is a jury?
3. Who was Subhadra?
4. What is special about the flag of Nepal?
5. Who was Friar Tuck?
6. What is Monopoly?
7. What is Sri Lanka's highest point called?
8. What is the clavicle in the human body?
9. How did the fax machine get its name?
10. Who was Aurangzeb?
11. What is an antenna?
12. What is an octopus?
13. What does an elephant use its trunk for?
14. In chess, what is the knight also called?

15. What is the composition of air?
16. Which are the letters not used by the World Meteorological Organization in naming Atlantic hurricanes?
17. What is special about the Tundra?
18. The Zambezi River gives its name to which country?
19. What is Ahmedabad?
20. What is actor Rajnikanth's real name?
21. What is the baby of a peafowl called?
22. In Great Britain, what is the name for a wet mixture of snow and rain?
23. What is henna?
24. What is Andhra Pradesh?
25. Who looked after Mowgli?
26. What are geysers?
27. What is smog?
28. Who was Ashoka?
29. What is Lake Superior famous for?
30. What is the name of the samadhi of former Deputy Prime Minister Jagjivan Ram?
31. Who is Mulk Raj Anand?
32. What are the three jewels of Jainism?
33. What is the French name for the English Channel?
34. Who was Juan Perón?
35. In 1604, who was appointed as the first keeper of the Guru Granth Sahib?
36. Who discovered the presence of the malarial parasite in the Anopheles mosquito?
37. Into what periods is the Stone Age divided ?
38. What do you call a large rally by a group of Scouts?
39. What is a fathom?
40. Name the island on which Napoleon was exiled.

41. What do you call the line on high mountains above which snow never melts.
42. What is New Zealand?
43. Who is Boutros Boutros-Ghali?
44. Who were the Mauryas?
45. What is candyfloss?
46. What is the flag of Cyprus?
47. In Great Britain, what do you call a four-sided plane figure with one pair of parallel sides?
48. What is another name for the Abominable Snowman?
49. What is the currency of Thailand?
50. What is ginger called in Hindi?

IQ

1. 2401. The consecutive exponents of the digit seven.
2. POD. RAN are the three central letters in the word CRANE, and POD are the central letters in the word SPODE.
3. 25 (Add the digits: 1+9+6+3+2+4=25, 3+2+9+1+3+7=25)
4. 54 (8x3=24, 13x 3=39, so 18x3=54)
5.

1	C	5	G
A	3	E	7

Every alternate letter starting from A and its numeric position in the alphabet is given.
6. NIROY (Irony). All the others are metals or alloys—Steel, Copper, Bronze.
7. William Shakespeare
8. Neither. When they meet they will be the same distance from Kolkata.

9. Three minutes
10. METOC (Comet—an airliner). The others are makes of cars—Ford, Bentley, Vanguard, Fiat.
11. APE
12. 9 (DRIVER has 6 letters +1 = 7, PEDESTRIAN has 10 letters + 1=11, ACCIDENT has 8 letters+1=9
13. 33 (2+1=3, 3+2=5,5+4=9, 9+8=17, 17+16=33)
14. 3=(4+4+4)/4
15. Birds=10, Animals=20
16. Yesterday
17. No
18. Ten (Each brother had the same sister)
19. There is no mud in a hole.
20. Sixteen
21. 99 (Beginning with 7, even multiples of 7 are added to the previous number to get the next number.)
22. EHOSU (House). The others are public places of worship—Temple, Church, Mosque.
23. Rohan. He came earlier as his watch was fast.
24. All yellow dogs need food.
25. In any book, pages 19 and 20 are two sides of the same page.
26. Two friends at the same time
27. 48 (Odd numbers from 5 onwards are added to get the next number.)
28. Four
29. 11:09
30. 27 (Two consecutive series are present. In the first series, each number is multiplied by 2 and in the second, by 3.)

SPEED ROUND

SET 1
1. Mango
2. Bi
3. Joking. She is Tanuja's daughter.
4. Tarot card
5. Eight
6. Rajiv Gandhi
7. Caps

SET 2
1. Quicklime
2. An ogre
3. Joking. It is a cake with a streaked or mottled appearance achieved by very lightly blending light and dark batter.
4. Imran Khan
5. Six
6. Nirvana
7. Bangladesh

SET 3
1. Four
2. Swami Vivekananda
3. India
4. Okapi
5. Umar Sheikh Mirza
6. Midas
7. Autograph

SET 4

1. Ehsaan
2. Serious
3. Himachal Pradesh
4. Velodrome
5. Eggs
6. Primary colour
7. Sanskrit

SET 5

1. Iron
2. Noodles
3. Delta
4. Ikkat
5. Monopoly
6. Ostrich
7. Joking. The music was composed by his son R.D. Burman.

SET 6

1. Irrawaddy
2. Omelette
3. Indra
4. Donald Bradman
5. Jawaharlal Nehru
6. Hero
7. New York City

SET 7

1. An apple
2. Holland; dykes are embankments built to prevent flooding from the sea

3. Oliver Twist
4. Dhol. The name of the dog is Dhole.
5. Arsenal
6. X-ray
7. Serious; Pakistan's population is 190,291,129 while Russia's is 138,082,178

SET 8

1. Australian Open; it is usually played in the month of January
2. *Jaws*
3. Varanasi
4. Uma Bharti
5. Orca
6. 011
7. Haley's Comet, after Edmund Haley

SET 9

1. India
2. Sarojini Naidu
3. Embassy
4. Tabu
5. Serious
6. Ashok Chakra
7. It increases.

SET 10

1. Mohammad Sami
2. Herbivorous
3. East
4. Ehrlich

5. Spout
6. Tipu Sultan
7. Zubin Mehta

SET 11
1. Left-handed batsman
2. Leo Tolstoy
3. Serious
4. Kunti
5. Neutron
6. Tamil Nadu
7. Mahima Choudhary

SET 12
1. Social
2. Nagpur
3. Gulf
4. Moon
5. India
6. Nobel
7. Greek

SET 13
1. Joking
2. Mohammad Kaif
3. Iguana
4. Rockies
5. Organization
6. Cochin
7. Antoine Lavoisier

SET 14

1. Electron
2. Madri
3. Peacock
4. Godavari
5. Pakistan
6. K
7. New Delhi

SET 15

1. One Day Internationals
2. Iridium
3. Nostradamus
4. Gujarat
5. Serious
6. *Sikander*
7. Shakuni

SET 16

1. Jane
2. Magnesium
3. Cauvery
4. Census
5. North
6. Termite
7. No ball

SET 17

1. Equine
2. Serious
3. Shah Jahan

4. Olive Oyl
5. K.S. Ranjitsinhji (1872–1933), who played Test cricket for England
6. Eat it or cook it.
7. They are cousins.

SET 18
1. Investigation
2. Squirrel
3. Ooty
4. Trim
5. Lleyton Hewitt (Twenty years old)
6. Albert Einstein
7. Rice

SET 19
1. Narmada
2. Conch shell
3. Arabic
4. Tipu Sultan
5. Tutti-frutti
6. Fathom
7. Sport

SET 20
1. Madhya Pradesh
2. Dino Morea
3. Japan
4. Asia
5. Yangon
6. Inch

7. Graffiti

SET 21
1. Half mast
2. Ounce
3. Rohtang
4. Romania
5. *Macbeth*
6. Naan
7. Akbar

SET 22
1. Mussoorie
2. Taxis
3. Serious
4. England
5. An oyster
6. Madhubani
7. C. Rajagopalachari

SET 23
1. Ten
2. Amitabh Bachchan
3. Secunderabad
4. Theyyam
5. Exit
6. Lungs
7. Agra

SET 24
1. Sourav Ganguly

2. Orange
3. Canada
4. Iodine
5. Euclid
6. Pizza
7. Mahatma Gandhi

SET 25
1. Sri Aurobindo
2. Lucknow
3. Copper
4. Jalebi
5. Orange
6. *Rubbaiyat*
7. Gilli danda

SET 26
1. Bhopal
2. None
3. Nandi
4. Nine
5. Egg
6. Bamboo
7. Black

SET 27
1. Pune
2. Gold
3. From
4. Europe
5. Compass

6. Cholas
7. Indira Gandhi

SET 28
1. Ganga
2. Snail
3. Joking
4. Spider-Man
5. South Africans
6. Anatomy
7. Mickey Mouse

SET 29
1. Andhra Pradesh
2. The sun
3. Joking; it was made from a pumpkin
4. Sixty
5. Nur Jahan
6. Shekhar Kapur
7. Pigeons

SET 30
1. Six
2. Joking; it is a ball and socket joint
3. Meghalaya
4. Amber
5. Chaitra
6. 2000 CE
7. Unidentified Flying Object

SET 31
1. Tamil
2. Jawaharlal Nehru
3. Pisa
4. Red
5. Larynx
6. North Pole
7. Fonts

SET 32
1. A pair
2. Joking
3. Draupadi
4. Four
5. Drive a car
6. Yeast
7. Blue

SET 33
1. Old things
2. Serious
3. Clutch
4. Leaves
5. Twenty-three
6. Mike Tyson
7. Adelaide

SET 34
1. Joking; it lies to the west
2. Freeze
3. Three

4. Alexander
5. Seventy minutes
6. White
7. Reverse

SET 35
1. Serious
2. Ribs
3. Margaret Thatcher
4. Four
5. Dhow
6. Three
7. Ring

SET 36
1. Rice
2. Horse
3. Night
4. Atlantic Ocean
5. Giraffe
6. Four
7. Implosion

SET 37
1. Vacuum
2. Salty
3. Small
4. Jawaharlal Nehru
5. Serious
6. Bees
7. Five

SET 38

1. *The Tempest*
2. Circumference
3. Nilgiris
4. Joking
5. Liver
6. Green
7. Numismatics

SET 39

1. Serious
2. Blue
3. Alan Shepard
4. Canada
5. Bal Gangadhar Tilak
6. Donald Duck
7. Crabs

SET 40

1. Joking; it is in New Delhi
2. Football
3. Helicopter
4. Six
5. The arteries
6. Weight
7. Hamelin

SET 41

1. The dish
2. Joking; he studies the atmosphere and weather
3. Egypt

4. Ikebana
5. Asia
6. Expand
7. A.R. Rahman

SET 42
1. White
2. Joking; he lost his vision by the age of five
3. Also in Maharashtra. Both are located in Mumbai.
4. The product
5. Arthur C. Clark
6. P.S.
7. Raj Kapoor

SET 43
1. Black
2. Australia
3. David Copperfield
4. Serious
5. Chalukyas
6. Nine
7. Beans

SET 44
1. Vexillology
2. Serious
3. Thirty
4. Extra (Extra Sensory Perception)
5. Arthur Conan Doyle
6. Percussion
7. Thank you

SET 45

1. 86,400
2. Mr Hyde
3. Joking; it is a male duck
4. Bhutan
5. Above
6. Five hours
7. Kapil Dev

SET 46

1. Indian Railways
2. Serious
3. 75 km
4. The Wright brothers
5. Your head
6. Rajesh Khanna
7. Siraj-ud-daulah

SET 47

1. Lotus
2. Serious
3. The summit or peak
4. A cat
5. Six
6. India
7. Bumstead

SET 48

1. Sputnik
2. Serious
3. Yamuna

4. The nose
5. Seven
6. Robin
7. There are none.

SET 49
1. Serious
2. The Qutb Minar
3. Sugriva
4. Shift
5. Dilip Kumar
6. Feet. It is a type of shoe.
7. Rugby

SET 50
1. George H.W. Bush
2. Serious
3. Australia
4. Seven
5. Appendix
6. The US
7. Karishma Kapoor

www.ingramcontent.com/pod-product-compliance
Lightning Source LLC
Chambersburg PA
CBHW030328020726
47493CB00004B/1199